MW00903456

Churlish Tales of
Nonsensical Sophistry

Churlish Tales of Nonsensical Sophistry

by
Winston Roberts

2017

Copyright © 2017 by Winston Roberts

All rights reserved. This book or any portion thereof may not be reproduced or used in any manner whatsoever without the express written permission of the publisher except for the use of brief quotations in a book review or scholarly journal.

First Printing: 2017

ISBN: 978-1-718-00022-3

Dedication

To Jackie, John and Lilli.

CHURLISH TALES OF NONSENSICAL SOPHISTRY

Cover art by Lillian Rosa

Contents

Monstrous Ailment

His visage in the mirror was off somehow. His eyes were bloodshot, but that didn't seem too unnatural. The furrows in his brow, while pronounced and deep, weren't that much deviated from the norm. His pallor was a chalky gray, which to his eye seemed a little chalkier than usual. He stuck out his tongue: blue and swollen. Finding this definite sign of illness, he donned his outer cloak and thick boots and headed for the Emergency Room.

The night was cold and a drizzle had started. He pulled his coat collar tight around his neck, in an attempt to keep more of his body warmth in the inside of the garment. The drizzle was dampening the fabric, and slowly the moisture penetrated through the coat and his shirt onto his skin. This wouldn't help whatever was wrong with him, he figured. He shivered and kept walking.

Finally, at the ER he strode to the counter and waited patiently for the nurse to acknowledge him. He wouldn't wait long. The angel of mercy behind the counter shoved a clipboard his way and uttered, "Fill this out." He took the board, with its pen attached, and headed for an open seat in the waiting area.

The ER wasn't full tonight, but it was full enough to see that he looked ill enough for people to choose the seats farthest away from him. A little boy sat next to him, only to have his mother whisk him away to generally recognized ER waiting room safety. He didn't mind; he must look a fright with his ashen pallor and blue tongue.

The form wanted some personal information. The first line wanted his name, and provided those willingly:

Last name: Stein

First name: Frank

Middle Initial: N

The rest of the document featured questions he either didn't understand or they didn't seem to apply. They asked for something called a Social Security Number. He figured that one person alone wasn't very comforting but that if a man had a friend to talk to then life could be very secure indeed. He put a '2' for that.

The question arose about something called health insurance. He didn't think he had any of that so he left it blank. In addition, there were a lot of other queries about health history, but this being his first illness, he didn't know if that applied. He left this blank also. Feeling he'd complied as best he could with the nurse's questionnaire, he turned in his clipboard and waited to be called. He didn't have to wait long.

"Mr. Stein." The nurse called out to the crowd in the waiting room.

Frank rose from his chair and approached the counter thrilled at his luck in having gotten in so fast.

"Mr. Stein." The nurse looked up at him above her glasses that she perched at the very end of her nose. "You don't have any health insurance?"

The question hit Frank as odd. He guessed the health insurance was more important than he had thought. "Ummm, no."

The nurse let out a sigh of exasperation, as if this wasn't the first time she had had to deal with this issue. "You need to go to the free clinic across town." She shuffled through some papers and produced a flyer describing the clinic, its purpose and its location. Frank took the flyer and slowly, persistently read the information.

It seemed to him that folks not possessing the health insurance had to be treated at the free clinic, and so it being the case that he had none, he would have to go there. That seemed obvious. That seemed like his fate, even though he was loathe to make the journey.

He left the ER and started walking. The drizzle had now turned to outright rain. His clothes were soaked, so no turning of the collar or pulling the coat over his head would help his situation. He trudged on in silent suffering.

A taxi cab rolled by him on the street, and hailing the driver as best he could, he failed to flag him down. As a matter of fact, the look the driver gave him made him feel that his illness may be progressing more rapidly; that his appearance may not inspire confidence in his fellows.

He had been worried for a while now that he might not be acceptable to society in general: that he may be some kind of misfit, some kind of pariah. But then he thought that there were so many apocalyptic movies, where infection had caused the destruction of society. Fear of contagion was in the communal psyche. That was the reason for his shunning, he told himself. It was the illness.

After hours of walking he arrived at the free clinic, chilled to his very bones. The nurse behind this counter gave him a similar clipboard full of similar questions to the ones he'd answered before. Being more experienced in the filling out of medical forms now, he raced through this one and returned it.

The waiting room here was more crowded than the other had been. There were several seriously injured and ill people here. He would gladly wait if those that were in urgent need could be helped first. He also didn't mind waiting, as the temperature in the room was nice and toasty. It wasn't long before his teeth stopped chattering and he could nap a bit.

He was awakened by a nurse bursting through the double doors at the end of the room and shouting, "Stein!"

He leapt to his feet and followed the nurse to a bed with a curtain pulled around it.

"Take off all you clothes and put this on." The nurse handed him a gown.

He was glad to remove his sodden clothing. He draped his clothes on the back of the chair located beside the bed. He unfolded the gown he had been given, and immediately noticed that it was not going to cover his 8 foot frame. He was even going to have trouble getting his arms through the arm holes. He decided finally to opt for tying the garment around his waist to hide his 'privates'. He didn't want to scare any children that might be lingering about.

He plopped himself onto the bed with his feet dangling over the end of the bed. He pulled the blanket up over his knees to just under his chin. It wasn't long and a doctor pulled back his curtain and introduced himself.

"Hello Mr. Stein. I am Doctor Shoemaker."

"Ummm. Hi." Frank rarely started any conversation without an 'Ummm' to begin.

"Now what seems to be the problem?"

Frank conveyed to the doctor his feelings of lethargy, his unnatural pallor and his tongue. The doctor quickly got out a tongue depressor and one of those teeny flashlights they use to look at your head and began to probe and prod the patient patient.

"Now, what explains these bolts on your neck?"

Frank thought that was obvious. "Ummm, hold head on body."

"Hmm, I noticed from the nurse's notes that you have a body temperature of 82 degrees. Is that normal for you?"

"Ummm, Frank guess so."

The doctor scratched his head and making a few notes in the chart vacated the ersatz room.

Frank didn't have to wait long. The doctor came back into his curtained sanctuary bringing a convoy of other doctors and residents. The group talked in subdued whispers, with one or the other taking a break to listen to Frank's heart or take a pulse. Finally Dr. Shoemaker spoke.

"Mr. Stein. We're not sure how to treat you. As far as we can tell, you should be dead. Even further, we think you may already be dead."

Frank didn't like this diagnosis. It was obvious to him that he wasn't dead and if these quacks didn't know that, how in the world were they going to heal him. It was time for him to go.

"Ummm, me go."

Frank donned his wet clothes and made his way out of the clinic and headed home.

Finally at home, Frank decided that what he really needed; what could not possibly hurt was a nice hot bath. He climbed the flight of stairs to his bathroom and ran the water. The water was running nice and steamy. It wasn't long before the entire bathroom was filled in a cloud of health giving fog.

'Ummm, make better with TV!' Frank thought to himself. He rummaged through the hall closet and finding an extension cord there, ran the power from his bedroom into the bathroom. A visit to his bedroom produced a small TV he used on occasion to help fall asleep, which he positioned on the bathroom vanity.

Frank threw his wet clothes into the hallway. He'd put them in the dryer later. It was time for comfort, and so dialing the TV to a rerun of the Honeymooners, Frank slowly, carefully lowered himself into the hot bath. Water spilled everywhere over the sides of the tub. The modern bathtub was small indeed but it was exceedingly too small for Frank. He placed his feet on the wall where the faucet lived, and his head rested on the wall opposite.

Jackie Gleason was in rare form in this episode. He was so mean to everyone, but he had such a big heart behind that. Ed Norton entered the scene and was teaching Ralph Cramden how to play golf with his usual joie de vivre. Ralph lost his temper and flailed at his TV friend. Frank found this so amusing he convulsed with laughter. The convulsion was his undoing, however, he knocked the vanity so hard with his foot, the TV teetered over the edge and then into his lap in the tub.

A short shower of lightning sparks filled the bathroom and then nothing but silence and blackness in the whole house.

The sun was just coming up over the horizon when the rain stopped. Inside this one particular house sat one particular man with a TV on his lap. His eyes were closed; his body limp. Suddenly, as if reborn, the man gasped for air, filling his lungs with the life giving oxygen. He sat upright. What had happened?

He pulled himself out of the tub, and going to the mirror, wiped the condensation from the glass to get a better look. What he saw delighted him. There in the mirror was a man with admittedly hair standing on end, and black char marks on his flesh, but his skin! His skin had assumed its normal greyish hue. He stuck out his tongue. I was a bright green again, and the small pink pustules were back with the fine little hairs on them! He admired what to him was a very handsome man in the mirror.

The bath had given him the jolt he needed. He was ready to rejoin polite society. His illness gone, he would be accepted for sure this time.

Diet Camp

The parking lot was filling up when he arrived. He navigated to a shady spot under a large pine tree and turned the key, quieting the engine. He grabbed his duffel bag with all of the necessaries he'd need for the week and strode to the welcoming, sign in area.

There were many other fatties (as he called his brethren) waiting in line. He pulled his paperwork from the pocket of his bag, and made a last check of their ultimate completion. When his turn presented itself, he stepped to the smiling lady at the table and handed her his forms.

"Well hello Walter!" The lady beamed with joy at discovering his name. "We've been expecting you!"

Walter, thinking that statement to be altogether too familiar, responded. "Umm, I prefer Walt." And then: "I've been expecting to be here too!" He gave the nice passive aggressive lady a smile and a wink.

After a back and forth over payment options and health issues he might have, the lady handed him a laminated badge that dangled at the end of a rather colorful lanyard. "OK, you're ready for the nurse now. She's at the table by the door." She pointed to a young lady in a nurse's uniform standing behind a table of pamphlets.

The nurse took down his medical history and he handed her his medications. She was responsible for seeing that he took them at the right times. Having completed her interrogation, she motioned to the scales sitting by the table. "OK, hop on."

Walt stepped onto the scales and sucked in his gut. Why he sucked in his gut, he didn't know; it wasn't going to change his weight in the slightest. The display window jumped up and down from the 350's to the 280's. His spirits dropped in the 350's and were buoyed back when the 280's appeared. Finally the device froze at a weight of 324. That seemed pretty typical to him. The nurse wrote the value in her notes and looking at his forms then to Walt said, "Cabin number 5." She rounded her lips in an expression of incredulity. "That's Hank's cabin! You'll love Hank!"

He took the lanyard he had gotten from the first lady and throwing it over his neck he picked up his bag and headed for the cabin. "Thanks!" He hoped he wouldn't end up despising Hank.

His doctor had recommended this camp for him. His weight was putting too much burden on his heart. The doctor warned that if he didn't do something about his excess poundage he probably wouldn't live to see his kids graduate from high school. That had woken him up, from his denial about his health.

Cabin 5 was the fifth and last cabin in the semicircle of cabins ringing the common area. The cabins looked identical with bunk beds on the right, and bathroom facilities on the left. Hank was already in the cabin when he arrived and greeted him. "Hello! Who have we got here?"

He was already loathing Hank. He was one of those cheerleader types; he could tell already. Hank would be the source of his suffering this week, no doubt. Walt extended his hand reluctantly. "Hello, I don't know who the 'we' are, or who they 'got', but I'm Walt." He smiled to lessen the blow of his acrid remark.

Having arrived late, Walt didn't get a lot of time to unpack. There was to be a big assembly in the common area to welcome the attendees. Walt grabbed a sweatshirt, as the sun was sinking and the temperature dropping. He made his way to the well-polished logs they used as benches around the camp fire. The fire was already ablaze in the middle of the bucolic amphitheater. Each cabin was encouraged to sit together.

The crowd grumbled with attendees greeting each other and making their connections. There were screams of joy as attendee found common interests with attendee. A gray haired man arose from one of the benches and, raising his arms, called the audience to silence.

"Welcome friends! I am your camp director, Dr. Williams." He smiled as he turned to regard each camper. "What a week we are going to have!"

Walt noticed two counselors approaching with arms full of clothing. They were apparently carrying t-shirts.

"Ah good. " Dr. Williams motioned for the counselors to pass the shirts around. "These are your uniforms for the week. Each cabin will compete with the others for the grand prize of Camp Winitoctoc's Dieters Extraordinaire!" There were oohs and aahs whisking through the crowd at that. "That's right, the cabin that loses the most weight, wins!" The campers roared their approval in shouts and applause.

Dr. Williams then proceeded to spell out the rules and regulations of the camp. No outside food permitted. If you were caught with contraband, you would be asked to leave. There were other privacy issues and various other dos and don'ts. What followed Dr. Williams' talk, was a cavalcade of counselor introductions with the entire proceedings ending with the camp nurse. Dr. Williams dismissed the affair and they all headed to the mess hall for dinner.

Well, they called it dinner, but to Walt it was more like a light snack. There were plenty of raw vegetables with some nasty tasting fish. The dinner's entertainment consisted of a talk on heathy food choices by one of the counselors, followed quickly on by the Emotional Side of Weight Gain, by Dr. Marvin Williams, PsyD.

After dinner and still hungry, but he knew he would be hungry, Walt trudged back to the cabin. He walked with his fellow campers. They had decided at dinner to call the cabin 5 crew, the Calorinators, in that they were there to terminate their calorie intake.

He walked with a large man, and a fellow Calorinator, named Glenn. Glenn had been given an ultimatum by his wife to get healthy or she would leave him. He said she was doing it for his own good, but Walt wondered if there might be some kind of underlying agenda. What a pitiful sap, he thought. Glenn's wife was probably in Vegas with the pool boy this week, thought Walt.

Back at the cabin, he wished Glenn a good night. Walt washed his face and brushed his teeth and taking his bedtime pee, lay down in his bunk and pulled the covers tight to his chin. It wasn't long before he had drifted off to sleep, the rigors of the day melting away.

Climbing steeply from a world of dreams, he awoke to utter bedlam. Hank was shaking a fellow cabin mate to consciousness as Walt rubbed his eyes, the better to see. Outside in the common area, through a haze of smoke, Walt could see campers congregating. Hank approached his bunk and with a frenzied looked implored him. "Get dressed, pack your stuff and get to the common area. Bring your blankets."

Walt was unsure what was going on but obeyed, as Hank didn't look like he was joking. At all. He dressed in a hurry and shoved all he could find into his duffel bag. He draped the blankets from his bunk on his shoulders. They would help keep him warm; the night's chill was in full flower.

Outside in the common area, Dr. Williams was talking to some kind of fire fighter with an official looking red helmet. Walt approached the pair and eavesdropped on their conversation. It seemed there was a forest fire brewing in the area and they would have to evacuate. There were other fire fighters directing campers to gather round. Dr. Williams explained.

"Folks, we have a situation here. There is a forest fire raging in the lower valley that is threatening our camp. All of the roads have been closed, so we are going to have to 'shelter in place' until the fire fighters can control the fire. We have a primitive shelter just three miles hike from here that where we can hunker down, if you will, until it's safe for us to evacuate. If you all will just follow your cabin leader we can start to make the trek to our new home."

Well that was just fine! Why did he spend the $1500 it cost to attend this fiasco, if he was just going to hide out in the woods? Walt pulled his blankets tighter around his shoulders and threw the strap of his bag over his shoulder and proceeded to join the herd migration to the 'primitive camp'.

He walked with his new friend Glenn. The hike through the woods was very slow going. Most of the campers were quickly out of breath and needed a rest. Walt and Glenn were no exceptions. They hiked for what must have been hours with no end in sight. There was more than one meltdown along the way. Most of these people had never ventured far from their recliners, including Walt. Walt leaned on his buddy Glenn. He felt as little guilty making Glenn work just that much harder. At the end of their 'trail of tears', you found many campers holding up other campers, as the group finally attained their destination.

The primitive camp lay beside the small river that ran through the valley. The camp boasted two open air shelters, each consisting of a long wooden platform, with a roof supported by large timber pillars. The habitats sported stone chimneys at one end for cooking. Picnic tables lined up in rows covered the platform area. The counselors instructed campers to set up their areas by cabins. Cabins 1 through 3 took the first shelter and 4 through 5 took the second. The second shelter would also house the administration and nursing staff.

It started to rain. The campers were encouraged to turn the picnic tables on end, where they could be used as a perimeter for their housing. This resulted in reducing the amount of wind and rain allowed inside the structure. There was a pile of firewood behind the shelters and a team of wood movers was formed for shelter 2 with Walt as their leader. Through a curtain of whining and general belly aching, the team managed to load the fireplace with wood and get it blazing. The campers now completely and totally exhausted, settled down for a miserable night. The cluster of blubber butts situated themselves as close to the fire as possible, and camper slept next to camper for warmth.

The morning dawned and, sleepy eyed, the camp roused to life. There was groaning and complaining, for sure, but times were tough and there seemed nothing anyone could do about it. Dr. Williams stepped into the campfire circle outside the shelters and encouraged the camp to convene.

"I've just now talked with the Fire Chief." All ears perked up at this news. "We are in for a rather prolonged stay as things look now."

Dr. Williams then went on to explain the details of the fire and the dangers of smoke inhalation and sudden wind changes. What was worse, and what instilled a lot of fear and panic into the group, was the fact that the roads were still closed and that their normal food supplier would not be able to make any deliveries. To top it off, all cell phone access was also down. The fire had taken the towers down. They were at the mercy of the inferno.

"There is good news, though." Ah, good news at last! "We had previously planned for an 'Edible Local Flora' field trip as one of the week's activities and so it is good luck that we have Hank Brewer with us. He's the leader of the Calorinators: cabin 5." Hank stood and waved to the crowd.

"Hank is a relative expert on the local flora here, and will be leading us on foraging excursions to see what we can find growing all around us." There were audible groans in response to this. Not only were they going have to eat weeds and twigs, they were going to have to go out and harvest them themselves.

"We also have some fishing equipment in the storage shed behind shelter 2 for those anglers in the group..." Dr. Williams pointed to the shed. "as well as rope and nets if anyone can think of a use for them." More groaning ensued.

The campers were in a bad mood. There was nothing that could be done for it, though. Two of the counselors arrived and to everyone's delight. They were carrying a bag of apples. "This is all we could salvage from the kitchen." Dr. Williams supervised the cutting and distribution of the apples.

Hank was organizing a foraging expedition and Walt's buddy Glenn was first in line. 'Of course he's the first!' Walt could have predicted Glenn's enthusiastic enlistment. Walt not having anything else to do, and at Glenn's insistence, reluctantly joined the search for food, sustenance and the American way. The boys were joined by a few more campers and cloth bags in hand, the team set out.

Hank was a wizard of the forest. He pointed out the different tree species as they hiked. He cautioned the eating of the Maclura ponifera, or 'horse apple' as it was commonly called. "Causes vomiting." That was enough to convince one to steer clear.

They happened on a spate of mushrooms. They collected morels and hen of the woods varieties. Diving further into the woods they found a pond, teeming with watercress. Hank advised the foragers, "Never harvest all of it; leave some for the forest."

An open field provided a bounty of dandelion greens and onion grass. They found clover and wild violets. Digging into the soil they uncovered wild radishes and yams. Having filled their bags, the group started back to camp when Hank spotted a particularly desirable find.

"Over here guys!" Hank stroked the leaves of a small tree he had found. "Sassafras! We can make tea from the roots!" The gathered round in a circle and began digging.

Back in camp, the explorers laid their bounty on the picnic tables in their shelter. Each shelter had been given the responsibility for collecting their own dinner. While they were gone, others had caught some fish, two small trout-like fish that somewhat resembled a largish minnow. One lady had found some fresh water clams and two crawdads on the river bottom.

They decided to boil the 'seafood' with the greens and onion grass. Someone had procured a handful of wild strawberries. They held those for 'desert' with their sassafras tea. Exhausted from the labors of the day, the campers convened by the fire circle as evening fell for sipping tea and for what some considered almost morally imperative, the singing of camp songs. Walt refused to sing: he felt it 'silly'. His guard was worn down, however, when someone started 'The Banana Boat Song'. It didn't take long before Walt was wailing the 'Day-O' lyric in full throat.

The week flew by with days spent foraging, gathering firewood and fishing. There wasn't much time or energy for much else. Each day Dr. Williams would report on the firefighting progress and each day the news came back better, but not yet. Finally, Friday came and they got the news that they could indeed return to their main camp. This news met with highly animated and boisterous applause.

The hike back was not much fun, but it seemed more endurable than the hike inbound. The way there was fraught with uncertainty, but now they were returning to civilization and hopefully more food!

Having reached the safety of their cabins and the cabin's relatively comfy bunks, the entire brigade collapsed for a nap. The camp administration relented any structure for this time and instead set up the common area for the final night's weigh-in.

The rest did Walt a world of good. He awoke with a newfound sunnier view of life. He grabbed his toiletries bag and headed for the showers. A bar of soap later, he emerged a new man, smelling of perfumed soap instead of his former funk. The common area was filling up, so he signaled his friend Glenn and got him motivated to move. The boys exited their cabin and found places in the great log semicircle of benches.

Dr. Williams called the camp to order and detailed the proceedings. Each camper would be brought up in turn to get their current weight, which would be subtracted from their weight taken at sign-in. The cabin with the best 'percentage weight loss' would be given the bragging rights along with a sugar free yogurt pop! The contest began.

Walt wasn't expecting much. He knew that they had been severely starved of calories this week, but how much weight he couldn't tell. Camper after camper stood on the scale and everyone lost something. The record by the time they had gotten to cabin 5 was 28 pounds. Glenn was called and stepping on the scale found out he had only lost 9 pounds. He was despondent until Dr. Williams told him that everyone loses weight at different rates at different times. It was your overall health that mattered.

Walt was next. He stepped on the scales and to his amazement he weighed 299 pounds! He had weighed 324 at the start, and so was thrilled with his 25 pound loss! It wasn't the record, but it was probably the most weight he had ever lost in one week.

Dr. Williams addressed the congregation. "Well we have had one heck of a week, haven't we!?" That was greeted with raucous applause and agreement.

"In a way I'm glad we had a fire this week." The campers hushed as they didn't think it was that pleasant.

"I am NOT glad for any that might have been hurt by the fire, but I am glad of two things. First, I think this week we learned just how little food it takes to sustain life." He paused to let that sink in. The majority had to agree. They really hadn't ever considered that they could live on leaves, twigs and minnows.

"Secondly, I feel like if I could survive a week like this, I am probably stronger than I think I am? " None could argue that either. Most thought they would be found dead and eaten by wolves. They had accomplished something they had heretofore probably thought impossible.

The results tallied: cabin 4 won the contest. They were Camp Winitoctoc's, Campers Extraordinaire. The counselors brought out some boxes of frozen treats and to everyone's delight, they all got one! There were no losers there that night, only the fat cells!

The next morning, Walt packed up, wished everyone goodbye and headed for his car. He paused on the way. Glenn's wife had come to pick him up. Glenn spotted Walt and motioned him over.

"Walt, meet Peaches."

"Hi!"

"Hello. Glenn tells me you were his rock this week!" Peaches beamed a smile as she hugged her man. "He lost 9 whole pounds! Look at him, there's hardly anything left of him!" She hugged Glenn like he had just come back from war. Glenn's kids ran up, back from exploring the camp. The children rushed into Glenn's arms. Glenn was lucky man.

Walt was taken aback by Peaches. He had assumed some pretty harsh things about Glenn's lovely bride. It occurred to Walt that maybe he had some judgmental attitude to lose along with the weight. Walt bid them well, and having already exchanged email info with Glenn, walked to his car and threw his duffel into the back seat. The engine fired, and Walt was on his way home.

He noticed the gas gauge on his dash and remembered he had to get gas. He stopped at a little gas station/convenience store just down the valley from the camp and filled up. Having topped the tank, he went inside to pay and get a cup of coffee. He approached the clerk with his Java and throwing some cash on the counter asked the man.

"You all seem to have survived the fire no problem!"

The clerk looked confused, "What's that?"

"The forest fire. This week…?"

"We ain't had no forest fire in this valley for over 20 years now." The clerk smiled and scratched his head. "It were a doozy, though." He handed Walt his change. "Have a good'n."

It was Walt's time to be confused, He walked to the guard rail that surrounded the gas station and looked out over the valley and up to Camp Winitoctoc. He could see nothing but pristine woodland, with no sign of a cinder let alone a fire. He couldn't even find a dead tree.

Then it dawned on him. "Those bastards!" His initial response of anger turned to rage. "How in the heck…" He bowed his head at the utter gall it had taken for them to have deceived them. To think of all the work foraging and all of the meager meals!

'But I saw the smoke the first night!' Walt was trying to piece it together. He guessed one could have done that with a camp fire, some green pine boughs and a large fan? Maybe they used smoke bombs?

He tried to recall Dr. Williams ever talking to any firefighters after day 1, but came up empty. Why he hadn't noticed that was a mystery. Maybe he was so calorie starved he couldn't think straight?

The more he thought about it, the more his rage subsided. It felt more like genius than subterfuge. What an elegant way to educate. Built in exercise too. What better way to get the entire camp moving and making healthy food choices!?

He decided that maybe he *could* forage at his local grocery store. He could 'fish' the seafood counter. It would be *way* easier than what they had been through this week. He just might even hike there, when he would go to the grocery store. He smiled. With all of the dandelions in his yard, just think of the savings on weed killer!

He put his car in 'drive' and headed home. He started laughing. "Those bastards!" The 'bastard' had become a term of endearment. Tears formed in his eyes. He was afraid he might have an accident he was laughing so hard. He had better get out of there before the forest fire overtook him!

Armadillo Paradise

He had made it to the smooth ground: the black ground with the white stripes down the middle. It was said that this ground was holy. The Creator had built the smooth ground to test the armadillos - to see who was worthy. Only the Chosen could make it to the other side.

He heard them coming before he saw them. They were fast moving boxes sitting on black round things. They whooshed by at amazing speeds. If you were caught on the smooth ground when one of them came, you were toast. He squinted his eyes as it passed; they kicked up a lot of sand as they went by.

He basked in the Texas summer heat. The sun was high in the sky and would give no succor to its searing flames. He liked the heat, it was much preferable to winter's chill. Another box was approaching. He could tell from the vibrations through his feet. It was a big one this time; one of those with 18 round black things. The ground shuddered as it passed. He hunched down to avoid being driven back by the wash the box threw on its way.

"Murph!" Murph was short for Murphy. It was his friend Al.

"Hey Al! How y'all doin'?" Al lumbered up beside him.

"Same-o. What y'all doin' here?" Al looked up and down the expanse of smooth ground to see if any boxes were approaching.

"Dunno. I might be thinkin' of making a run."

Al looked at Murph with suspicious countenance. "You crazy?"

Murph expected this response. How many of their friends and family had lost their lives trying to make the other side of the smooth ground? Murph turned to Al and smiled. "Maybe."

Murph went on to explain himself. "The old ones tell tales of the other side of the smooth ground. They say that there was a time when the smooth ground didn't exist. Armadillos could travel from here to there unimpeded. The land beyond the smooth ground has a river of water running through it with trees lining the sides. "

"That's just an ole campfire tale!" Al was not a believer.

"They say that when the fruit trees by the river drop their fruit they are covered in the fattest, juiciest maggots. The beetles are so round you can't eat them in one bite. They say that years ago one of the Armadillos over there made it here. He got curious as to what was over that there smooth ground and made it all the way here. And what's more..." Murph paused for effect, looking over his shoulder to make sure they weren't heard. "They have ladies!"

"Well if you ain't just the biggest armor plated idgit in the whole entire world!" Al laughed at his friend. "There ain't no sech thing!"

"There are to!" Murph was getting a bit peeved at his buddy.

"That's just a horse barn of hooey! Besides, we got us some fine ladies here!"

It was Murph's turn to laugh. "What, old lady Turnbull? She's so old she got dinosaur teeth marks on her shell!"

"What about Daisy? Daisy would be quite a catch."

"She's got a boyfriend, and he's a real donkey's ass!"

Al had to admit that Daisy's boyfriend, Richie, was a bit of a halfwit. "Well there's always Amy."

Al was reaching now.

"Amy's nice but what she got growing between her toes? Looks like leprosy or somethin'!" Murph made that face that armadillos make when they smell something unsavory. "Admit it, there just ain't no good prospects for us on this side of the smooth." Al nodded his head in agreement.

Murph lowered his voice and, in whispered tones, confessed. "I'm lonely Al. I want the wife and a den under the big live oak. I want to watch the kids playing in the grass, chasing the grasshoppers."

Al bumped his friend with his shell. "Well you always got me, buddy."

Murph sighed the sigh of a being resigned to a fate they had not wanted. "Yeah, but I'm not sure I'm ready to go full on homodillo."

Al chuckled. "Yep, you right. I don't think you got the fashion sense for that."

They both laughed.

The boys sat in silence watching the boxes roar by them, some going this way, some that. Finally Al broke their reverie. "Hey, ain't that Ernie over there?"

Murph nodded agreement. "Hey, Ernie!"

"I don't think he heard you … ERNIE!" Ernie either didn't hear them or he was ignoring them. The boys sat with rapt attention as they watched Ernie flip his head this way and then the other, waiting for his opportunity to make his run.

"I think he's going to run!" Murph turned to Al, excited and concerned at the same time. Ernie flexed his muscles in his legs and in one great leap jumped onto the smooth ground. Simultaneous to Ernie's leap, Murph felt the telltale vibrations in his feet. A box was coming!

"Ernie, BOX!" The boys shouted with all of their lungs. They needn't have wasted their breath, though. Ernie already knew he was in trouble. Ernie froze and then in a tragic failure of decision making, turned to return to their side of the smooth ground.

"Roll, Erine, ROLL!" Al knew he could roll faster than run.

Ernie grabbed his hind feet with his front feet and started his roll to the side when, in a mighty whoosh, the box ran over him. It had been one of the 18 round black things boxes.

Murph and Al ran to their friend's aid. What awaited them was the silhouette of what had been Ernie, but in a much wider, flatter form. The boys sat by the smooth ground for quite a while, silent in reverent reflection of the loss they had just taken.

"Well at least he tried." Murph was trying to find the positive.

"We never know when it be our turn." Al wiped some moisture from his eyes.

The boys turned to leave. Al swished his tail at Murph. "Hey! You wanna go down by the cactus garden? I found a coupla crickets there t'other day."

"Sure, I guess." Murph was shaken. Suppose that had been him instead of Ernie. "No fire ants, though. I've still got indigestion from them we had yesterday."

The duo waddled off into a gorgeous sunset. The quest for Armadillo paradise would have to wait for another day.

Dog and Tony Show

"Hey Joe!"

You'd think that was a normal way to start a story, but you'd be wrong. You'll be surprised when you find out. The 'Hey Joe!' above was anything but normal. In fact, some would call it somewhat eerie.

"Hey Max!"

That this one is much more pedestrian will become obvious. The 'Hey Max!' above could have been said in the fanciest concert halls of the fanciest European cities and not have raised an eye brow. Not that being European puts a stamp of normalcy on anything. In fact, one could have said it at the White House and all would have approved.

"Why don't you jump up here and I'll comb the brambles out of your hair."

OK, so we are getting seriously out in the weeds now, both literally and figuratively. Why would Joe want to comb his friend's, nay, his BEST friend's hair? Were they married? Did Joe put the brambles in there? So many questions to answer.

All right, so it's time to let the cat out of the bag. But it's not a cat, but rather a dog. Max was Joe's dog. His BFF. Joe had raised Max from a puppy and it wasn't long until Joe heard Max making those weird sounds that eventually came to be speech. Speech like you and I speak. He spoke. He spoke English.

Max was a mutt. He had no pedigree to speak of, save maybe a predominant strain of Shetland Sheepdog. His long hair made the summers unbearable for him, being as Joe lived in the southern climes. He made Joe cut his beautiful long hair in April. It grew back by September.

Being able to talk to his friend made Max and Joe inseparable. Max was Joe's confidant, his ally, his wingman. They had devised a stratagem whereby Max would befriend the dog of the girl Joe thought he would like to meet. When the friendship between dogs was cemented, Joe would enter the scene and apologize for his dog's rude behavior. The strategy worked most times.

One particular time, the boys (and Joe thought of Max as just one of his 'boys') were playing catch the Frisbee at the dog park when Joe spotted a young lady sitting on one of the benches with her dog friend lying beside.

Joe turned to Max. "How about those two?"

Max gave the ladies a gander and then back to Joe said, "That one's a dog!"

Joe sighed the sigh of a man tired of the same old excuses. "Of course she's a dog, that's the point isn't it?"

"I know she's a dog, but really now look closer. She's a *dog*."

"When have you ever been choosy?" Joe knew his buddy well.

"Yeah, I guess you're right. I'm a real dog, when it comes to bitches." Max said this sarcastically.

Now Max had not said something unsavory; quite the contrary. Max's declaration of his predilection toward members of the opposite gender of his species was indeed correct in usage and syntax. His phraseology and terminology would be acceptable in even the most hallowed halls of the National Kennel Club.

Max felt as if his talents were wasted. His mental gymnastics ran to: 'I mean, a talking dog and all you can do is use him as a wingman?' Joe kept assuring him, though, that once it was publically known that he could talk, his life would pretty much not be his own anymore.

Max trotted over to the resting pair and, making the proper obligatory, perfunctory sniffing introductions, eventually settled down to nap with his new lady. He tactically placed his head on the stomach of the girl dog, and gave the human lady his best sad eyes routine.

Phase One of the mission complete, Joe scurried over and with profuse apologies explained that his dog was just overly friendly. He furthered that the beast didn't know the limits of human social niceties. The lady could rest assured that the hound would be properly and summarily berated upon getting him home.

Well, the apology was so well given, and the young man before the lady was not too unpleasant on the eyes. The nice lady having done her deliberation, invited Joe to sit awhile and let the two dogs discover their romance. Joe winked at Max. They were 'in'.

The lady's name was Katie, and her dog, Dory. That should have been the first red flag. Why would anyone name their dog after a fish? They tried to make a relationship out of it, but it wasn't long before both Katie and Joe were fed up with each other. Katie wanted someone more stable; Joe had a hard time holding a job. To Joe, Katie was something of a bitc ... umm ... let's just say Joe thought Katie was a 'bit' of a complainer.

Katie had a point about Joe. He really cycled from job to job. He had dropped out of college, and, the economy being what it was, had to take some of the more menial positions available in the market. He tried being a barista like most of his hipster brethren, but the constant kowtowing to the 'customer' left a bad taste in his mouth. In fact, a lot of his problems with gainful employment centered on his lack of interest in pleasing *anyone*, be they customer, manager or co-worker. Joe found that few people had the time or inclination to treat the members of the lower strata of the workforce with deference.

Being between jobs gave Joe a lot of time to think. He was reclined on his sofa in a day dream, when all of a sudden he snapped to life. "Max!"

Max, having just been wrested from his mid-morning nap, shook his head to clear the cobwebs and answered his friend, "What in tarn hill is so important as to disturb my nap!?" He sidled up to the couch and sat down.

"I've solved our money problems!" Joe beamed with confidence at the genius of his plan. "We're going to form a ventriloquism act!"

Now Max knew what ventriloquism was and he knew Joe didn't have the talent to pull that off. "How are you gonna do that with no training or experience in the ventriloquistic arts?"

"That's the beauty of it!" Joe paused for effect. "You already can speak."

Max let that sink in. Of course he could speak. "How is that ventriloquism if you're speaking and I'm speaking?" What a dumb idea.

"Because while *you* are speaking, I'll be pretending to not mouth your words!" Joe had his eyes wide open with rapt anticipation of Max's comprehension of the plan.

"I see." Max nodded his head. "You and I talk but the crowd is never going to buy that it's me talking. You pretend to be the ventriloquist." Max nodded some more. "Sounds like a good way for me to end up in a government missile silo somewhere, with my guts hanging out as they try to find what makes me talk." Max waited for Joe to say something soothing, reassuring. It did not come.

"No guts, no glory!" Joe smiled.

The boys set to developing their routine. Max wanted the material to be a little more bawdy than Joe. They settled on a middle ground of sorts.

"OK, so You'll say, 'Well if you didn't send so much time doing whatever it is you do in the shower, (pause for effect) you'd have more time to get my breakfast going in the morning.'" Max would then give the audience reality masking bark.

"And then Joe would say, 'If you didn't spend so much time licking your butt you would see the need for a shower.'"

The boys laughed.

Joe spent the better part of a day on the phone. As night was dropping in their world, Joe called to Max, "We've got a talent agent!" All that was left was to wait for the calls to come in from their agent. They would be on easy street in no time!

The agent booked their act at a local bowling alley. They would be the Saturday night 'draw'; to bring the people in to bowl. The guys setup at one end of the alleys. Joe tested the mikes and, to his surprise, found that Max's mike wasn't even plugged in. He called the kid, who was working the sound board, over.

"Hey. The dog's mike isn't live."

"Yeah." The teen didn't see the problem.

Joe sighed rather loudly. "Look." He paused to gather his thoughts and design a lie subtle enough to both convince the kid to plug the mike in, and at the same time not give away the act's little secret. "We're artists here. We need the mike open for out artistic integrity."

"Artistic integrity?" The boy didn't seem to understand why anyone performing at a bowling alley would have any integrity at all.

"Yes." Joe was losing the kid. "And the dog barks at certain times in the act."

The young man bought that one. He ran the necessary cables and hooked the mike live. Eight o'clock ticked off on the clock behind them and the boys started their act.

The sound of the pins falling as the patrons bowled was deafening. Joe could hardly hear Max. He wondered if the audience who, to all accounts, looked disinterested in whatever they were doing, could hear as well. The boys did their shtick. They received tepid applause, from the few who were waiting for their time to bowl and therefore had nothing to do but check them out.

They were the warm up act for the band. They packed their meager kit and headed for the manager to get their pay. "Two hundred dollars for 30 minutes of work!" Joe reached to high five his friend. It ended in an unenthusiastic low five from Max. The band took the stage and the bowlers erupted with cheers and applause.

"Man that was brutal!" Max started the performance debrief.

"Yeah, what a braindead crowd!" Joe paused in thought. "Maybe we need to dress you up in a tutu or something?"

"Tutu!? No effing way dude!" Max had his standards.

Joe called his agent to see if he had any feedback on their gig. He had to leave a message but on the ride home, they got a call.

"Hello."

"Hi Joe. How are you and Max feeling after your debut performance?"

"Well they didn't clap a lot. I'm thinking we may need to dress Max up a bit to give the act more pizazz!?" The phone went silent.

"That's a great idea!" Joe's agent cleared his throat. "What about adding an animal?"

"Add an animal?" Joe was confused how he could do the voice for another animal, given as how he wasn't actually doing the voice for the one they had now. "How would that work?"

"Well, Joe." The agent lowered his voice into a fatherly register. "It's just that there isn't all that much work available for ventriloquists. Folks are kind of over that." He let that sink in. "But, animal acts are very popular. I can book you two or three gigs right this minute as an animal act, but I'm afraid it's slim pickin's for the act you have now."

Joe thanked the agent and hung up. He scratched his head. "I guess we'll have to get another dog for the act."

Max wasn't having it. "Where are you going to get another dog that talks? Most of them can't even do simple math!"

The boys sat the rest of the ride home in silence.

The next day, Joe burst through their apartment door with a large pet carrier draped from his right arm. "Max come here! See what I got!"

Max trotted into the room and before he could ask, Joe produced a small orange pile of rags from the carrier. "His name is Tony!"

Max approached and sniffed the beast. It was really smelly. "What the heck is it?"

"It's a baby orangutan!" Joe beamed with pride as his acquisition. "I got it off of Craig's List!"

"Well…" Max was at a loss as to what to say. "How is this pile of hair and stink gonna help our act?"

"I'll teach him. Don't you worry."

They spent the week training Tony to do simple actions when prompted. They succeeded in getting him to turn his lips inside out to indicate his displeasure when Max insulted him on stage. They got him to ride on Max's back. The act was shaping up. They were going to be a hit for sure!

Their agent booked them a gig at a Shriners meeting. They would be the after dinner entertainment. The set up their equipment properly with Max's mike electronically enlivened. They combed Tony's hair as best they could, and feeling like all was right, they took the stage.

Tony was an instant sensation. The baby great ape performed the tricks they rehearsed aptly, but it was his improvisation that really got the crowd going. He climbed on Max's back but instead of riding him like a horse, like they rehearsed, he jumped up and down on poor Max, screeching all the while. The crowd roared! Max fumed.

The end of their act arrived and the boys took their bows. Joe and Max received polite applause, but when Tony's time came the house erupted. Max and Joe watched while their new addition to the group milked the audience in a shameful display of exploitation.

"What the eff was that!" Max was livid. "I'm a freaking dog that can *talk*! And this mindless orange bag of sh*t gets the standing ovation!?"

Joe shook his head. "There's no accounting for taste I guess?" He struggled for words. "They don't know it's *you* talking afterall?"

Max was inconsolable. The trio continued to perform at car dealership openings, and birthday parties. Tony grew ever increasingly incorrigible, with the crowds reacting ever more strongly with each outrageous antic. All the while, Max plotted his revenge. He wasn't going to let that upstaging little prima donna get away with it.

One night, while Joe slept, Max quietly crept into the living room of their small apartment. Slowly but surely, he pushed the latch of the pet carrier to the unlocked position and swung the metal door open. His foe lay sleeping inside, but when Max nudged him with his nose the monster awoke. The baby ape grabbed onto Max in his semi-sleep state and hung on like Max was his mother.

Max wasn't swayed by the ersatz display of affection. He had a plan. He drug the orange object of his rage to the window, and unlatching that, threw the little guy out. He closed and relatched the window, and then with a semi-clear conscience lay his head to rest at the end of Joe's bed.

The next morning, Joe turned on the TV while making the breakfast. The news was all atwitter with the story about the older woman who had been brought back from the brink of suicide by a baby orangutan. She had been sitting at her window with the pills laid out on the table, when the little guy had appeared. Her apartment being so high up, she feared the ape would fall and get hurt, so she opened her window. She not only opened the window of her apartment; she opened the window of her heart.

"Perfect!" Max couldn't believe it.

"Tony?" Joe couldn't believe it either.

Well Tony went on to have a great life. There were magazine covers and TV interviews. He gained so much in notoriety, that a major political party ran him for Mayor of New York. He won. There was even talk of running him for the presidency.

Joe went back to semi-working for a living. He was proud of the success he and Max had had with Tony, but it had really been a lot of work.

Max went on to write a book entitled 'Let me speak.' It was a biography or sorts, but contained no reference to the author's genetic pedigree. There was initially a chapter labelled 'Tony', but Max couldn't seem to finish it without ripping up the pages on which it was written. He shopped the book around to the publishing houses but they all passed. No one wanted a biography from a failed ventriloquist dummy it seemed.

Bunker Down

That did it. He had HAD it. He punched the power button on the TV remote and threw the device on the coffee table. The nightly newscast hadn't given much succor. More terrorism, more political corruption, more shootings, more embezzlement, more rape, more global warming, more of everything. Mankind was entering the terminal phase of his existence on this planet. He had to protect himself.

He got up early the next day. He headed for his bank. He would take out a second mortgage on his house: as much as they would give him; he would need money. The branch manager was a man in his middle age, with a steely eyed visage and firm handshake. He would have to talk fast to get this bugger to move on his loan. Thirty minutes later, he was out the door of the bank with loan secured.

His next stop was the heavy equipment rental establishment. He finagled the renting of a small bulldozer and excavator. He even arranged for them to deliver them to his back yard. He drove home and waited with great anticipation the arrival of his rented machinery.

With the bulldozer and excavator he was able to carve out a rather large hole in his backyard, piling the diggings high around the yard's perimeter. When he completed the hole to his satisfaction, he admired his work. The hole was appropriately deep, wide and long for his purpose. He dug a field for his septic system. Finished with the digging, he went to find a concrete company.

It took days for him to bend and entwine enough steel rebar to facilitate the concrete pour he envisioned. He wanted at least 3 feet for concrete floor and three feet of concrete wall. He would use extra rebar to make sure the high strength concrete he had requested would make the walls as durable as he could engineer. He hammered together walls of plywood sheets to hold the concrete together while it cured. The roof would come later.

The prep work complete, he called the concrete company to begin the pour. Truck after truck backed up to his little back yard and dumped their loads into his forms. Slowly and surely the floor and walls began to take shape. He used a 2x4 plank to probe the mix; to make sure there were no bubbles in the final product. Bubbles would weaken the result. He needed strong barriers to prevent unwanted guests entering this project he was building.

He waited for a month for the concrete to cure properly. He had time, he figured, and he wanted the structure as hard and sound as he could make it.

Next on his list was the drilling company that would perform the well drilling. They sent their truck to the site and, at his insistence, drilled not one, but a second deeper well also. He wanted the second deeper well should the first ever dry up.

He bought some 500 gallon septic tanks and installed those in the field he had dug previously just for this purpose. He laid the tanks in their gravelly graves and connected them to the concrete structure via underground PVC pipes.

The bulk of the underground systems in place, it was time to put on the roof. He built a temporary wooden roof structure over the box he had in the ground. The roof was six feet under the level of the original back yard. He wove 3 feet of steel rebar on top of that, and with many more trucks of high strength concrete, he finally had the basics of his 'end of the world' bunker. Backfilling with dirt to reach ground level, he finished the roof with grass seed on top.

He would outfit the bunker with solar paneling for electricity, but he was conflicted how to do the air handling. He may have to live in the bunker for years, depending on which direction the fall of society took. He would need fresh air.

He decided on an air cleaning system that could take 99.9% of particles out of the air. He then would pass that air through a series of filters to try and trap any other nasty compounds, be they radioactive or be they chemically toxic. He didn't need a fast flow through for the system, it was just he himself after all.

He would need all kinds of testing equipment, for the air especially, but also for his well water. He would need redundant systems too, it would be hard getting 'parts' during an apocalypse.

He mapped out the rooms he would need to build. He really didn't need to partition the space with walls as he was the only occupant, but he reasoned that it might break up the monotony of the space if he had different venues to occupy. He could reconfigure rooms as necessary, as needs arose.

He decided on one bedroom, one bathroom, one kitchen area, one living area, two mechanical systems areas and a storage area. He wanted two mechanical systems areas to separate water systems from air and electric. It seemed prudent.

He finished the interior with pine board paneling. It gave the place a rugged, classic look, sort of a cabin in the woods feel. He carpeted the bedroom and tiled the kitchen and bathroom. He left the storage room and mechanical rooms with their concrete floors. He decided to give the living area a wood flooring. He decided not to stain the floor. He thought the blonder hue would reflect more light, as there were no windows in the bunker.

Finding the inside of the bunker acceptable if not fully finished, he turned his attention to the outside security issues. In a breakdown of society, he would need to protect himself from the people who had not prepared for this eventuality. They would be storming his door trying to gain access and/or trying to get at his supplies.

A trip to the home store provided a pickup truck full of thorn bushes. He would plant these around the perimeter of the bunker to deter initial investigation of his site. All of the air intake and solar cells would be arrayed in the center of the bushes. With enough growth in the bushes, they might prevent intruders altogether.

He wasn't about to depend on the bushes for his security, though. He would need a strong metal door. No, that was wrong, he would need two metal doors. He searched and searched, but could not find anything thick enough to suit his expectations. He finally decided he would modify a vault door.

He would make his entry somewhat like a safe, but there would be no combination lock on the face. The door would be locked to the world by a simple latch and locker room lock, to keep the neighborhood kids from being curious. But when inside the bunker he would bolt the first door tight with a system of lock guards that fed through the internal door into the walls where the door was installed.

The second entry door would be similar to the outer one, save that it would possess a bullet proof glass window and a slot. The window was there to assess the danger without and the slot was for his pistol or shotgun.

His bramble of thorn bushes was thriving in their new home. He knew there was a bunker in the middle of the bushes but he couldn't see it. The air handling, water, sewage and electric systems seemed to be working fine. It was time to provision the bunker. Nothing on the news was reassuring him things were getting better.

The first order of business was to move all of the required furnishings from his house to the bunker. He cut a hole in one of the thorn bushes to allow access. He brought a bed, a sofa, a dining room table, some end tables and his entertainment system to his underground lair. He emptied his pantry and bathrooms of all of their food, chemicals, creams, medicines and soaps. He would have to launder his clothing in the kitchen sink, there were not enough resources in his end of the world house to accommodate a washing machine.

He secreted his pistol and rifles in the gun cabinet he had made in the living area, and filled to capacity the ammunition shelves above it. He left his pump shotgun with shells by the second entry door to repel any unwanted visitors.

The house now empty of everything useful he turned to the wholesale club to fill the storage area with food. It took two days to buy and carry enough 5 gallon jugs of water into the bunker. He knew water was heavy, but stockpiling years' worth of drinking water proved a gargantuan task. He would need the water in case the wells got befouled with any toxins.

Next on the list was the pharmacy. He stocked up on anything he could find over the counter that didn't require a prescription. He bought first aid supplies. He loaded a shopping cart with vitamins and dental care items.

He wasn't finished. The canned and dried food aisles got a visit. He loaded up 50 pound bags of rice. He bought dried beans,

beef jerky, powdered eggs, powdered milk and dried soup. He
bought anything canned he could find. Variety would be his friend
after a couple of years underground, he figured. He needed protein
so canned tuna and chicken were purchased in abundance, along
with every nut they displayed.

The task almost finished, he decided to get some of the less
necessary food stuffs like candy and gum. He found a 5 gallon
bucket of peanut M&M's. He loved peanut M&M's.

His checking account balance near zero and his credit cards
maxed out, he stuffed the remaining purchases into his bunker. The
overflow of goods spewed out of his storage area into the living
room. Every kitchen cabinet was stuffed to the gills. He had to
resort to storing his toilet paper hoard in his bedroom. It made going
in and out of the room a little cumbersome, but he anticipated that
problem getting less and less the more years that went by.

He was ready. He stood on the precipice of his creation and
looked around for a minute. This would be his last look at blue sky
for a while. He drunk it in. He stuffed some of the thorn bush
cuttings that he had made to allow access for his provisioning to
complete the exterior defense. All finished, he entered his
apocalyptic survival chamber.

He swung the outer door of the bunker shut and using the
wheel installed in the middle of the door, clicked the locking rods
into place. The rods ringed the door and made a very secure, rather
hard to defeat physical security measure. He walked the two steps
inside the bunker and swung the second door shut. It also had a
locking wheel, which he proceeded to actuate to give his secondary
fall back measure its life.

The batteries were on full charge so he decided to splurge and
put on two lights in the living area. He was hungry from his labors,

so he fired up the propane stove and started heating a can of Dinty Moore. He felt a tingle shoot down his left arm as he stirred the bubbling contents on the stove. He must be in quite an ebullient state of mind to get that tingling, he mused.

He served his hot dinner on his dining room table. The tingling he had felt in the kitchen had now escalated into a rather uncomfortable pain. He paused to massage his arm. Maybe he had strained the muscles carrying all of the stuff he had carried into the bunker. The massage proved no help.

Just as he was going to try and forget the pain and eat his dinner, he felt like a Rhinoceros butted him in his chest. The pain was excruciating. The Rhino then metaphorically sat on his chest as he fell to the ground, knocking his dinner on the floor with him.

Seven seconds later, he was dead.

Every Day Problem

Myra Dunwoody's glass wasn't half full, it was full to overflowing. She wasn't immune to the depressing and darker side of life; she was just not interested in letting it influence how she lived. She was a constant source of comfort for those who had the privilege of being around her. She made everybody she encountered, if not happier, less unhappy.

Myra had risen through the ranks at the IGA to become an Assistant Manager. She was being groomed to perhaps be given her own store to manage. They were building a new store on the other side of the state and, when finished, she would take the reins there.

Myra's team both loved and respected her. She tolerated no back talk and expected her team to perform to its ability. She was not blind to the personal problems of her crew, however, and could be counted on to bend the rules when needed, to accommodate.

Friday payday fell on their IGA slice of capitalistic enterprise, and, the big boss out for a conference at corporate headquarters, left Myra in charge. The store was full of customers filling up their baskets with goodies for the holiday weekend. Moms drug kids in their wake, and elderly couples stopped the flow of traffic at times reading the labels, checking the prices and adjusting their spectacles.

Myra's joy at the IGA was walking the floor to interact with the customers and staff. She walked through the produce aisle and encouraged Jimmy to restack the oranges. They looked sloppy. She visited the Deli counter to ask how Sylvia was doing with her new baby. She helped one of their elderly clients get a product from the top shelf in the bread aisle.

Over the store PA system, Carol from accounting paged Myra to her office, and just having solved a possible coupon fiasco, Myra headed there. She opened the door to her sanctuary and to her surprise found Carol sitting in a chair next to two gunmen carrying pistols. The men were dressed in jeans. They both wore a scarf over their faces. One had on a hoodie with the hood covering his head. The other had opted to use a skull cap to camouflage his head.

"What's going on!?" Myra was outraged at this confusing scene.

"Open the safe and no one gets hurt!" The taller of the two men put his gun in the middle of her back and shoved her toward the store safe that was mounted to the wall of her office.

"Ok, no problem, no problem." Myra was not going to jeopardize any of her team for any amount of money.

The men worked in unison, one held their duffel bag open while the other stuffed the cash inside. "Where's' the rest of it!?"

Myra could tell these were amateurs. They had no concept of how much cash a grocery carried now that most folks just used their credit cards to pay for their food, that, and the pervasive nervousness and apprehension in the men. "That's it. Credit cards, you know."

The men gave each other an anxious glance. They argued briefly then decided to exit the premises. "You're going with us." They motioned for Myra to lead them out of the store through the back door.

Myra stepped along in time with the robbers, not wanting to upset them. They were wired very tight as it was. The trio reached the getaway van parked behind the store and the tall man ordered the shorter one to "Put her in the back." The short man pushed Myra to get her started toward the back of the van.

Now Myra knew that her chances of surviving this episode would be reduced if she got into the van. These guys were novices with a high level state of agitation. There was no telling what they were capable of doing. If they were stupid enough to rob a grocery store in broad daylight, they were capable to do all kinds of stupid.

When the men had cased the store, they had considered making their move when the big boss was away. The Assistant Manager being a woman would simplify the process they presumed. What they didn't know was that Staff Sergeant Myra Dunwoody was the veteran of four tours of duty in Iraq and Afghanistan. Myra, a decorated and hardened soldier, had stared deeply into the eyes of her own mortality on many occasions.

Myra waited until the tall one moved to the driver's side to start the car, when she brought her fist down with as much force as she could muster onto the forearm of the shorter man. The strength of the blow caused the man to release his grip on his gun, letting it fall to the ground. The blow also was sufficient to crack the radius bone in the man's forearm, which was evidenced by the moaning the man exhibited as he clenched his forearm with his left hand. To insure the man's impotence in their short encounter, Myra struck a massive arcing swinging blow from her foot to the man's groin. The man buckled in pain to the ground.

Myra picked up the fallen pistol in time for the driver of the van to come around the corner to investigate. Myra debated with herself for a split second the use of the bullet in the chamber, or the use of the gun as a weight. She opted for the latter, slamming the butt of the pistol into the nose of the oncoming assailant. There was an immediate flow of blood from the nostril area and hearing the crack as the pistol hit its mark, Myra knew the nose to be broken. The tall man fell like so much lumber from the blow, either unconscious on the way down or made unconscious when his head hit the pavement.

Myra positioned herself with her knee in the small of the back of the short man. She fished her phone out of her pocket and dialed 911. Convinced the police were responding, she endeavored to field strip the gunmen's weapons. Her time in the Army had given her exceptional skill in the disassembly and reassembly of a weapon. She did it almost without thinking. Pulling the clips from the guns and clicking the round out of the chamber first, Myra proceeded to dismantle the metallic instruments of deadly force. She wanted the weapons neutralized for safety, and also so the police wouldn't get confused as to who was the perp and who was the victim. She sprinkled the pistol pieces in a pile on the asphalt.

The police arrived, along with a crowd of people who had heard about the commotion from the back lot. Four patrol cars arrived leading two ambulances. The police officers quickly controlled the scene and, after a quick assessment, incredulously calculated Myra as the victim. Myra was then interviewed by two separate officers. They wanted her to accompany them downtown for further questioning, but Myra convinced them to allow her to see them after her shift. She had a store to run.

Myra reentered her role in the store to an outpouring of applause and cheers. She nodded her head in acknowledgement of the praise and motioned for a return to normalcy with outstretched hands. She walked to her front line supervisor and asked. "Anyone hurt?"

"Janey's a little rattled." The supervisor pointed to a small 90 pound young lady shivering behind her cash register.

Myra approached the young girl. She was a favorite of the customers. She always had a bright smile and a kind word. Myra turned to a group of the stick crew mulling about. "Ask the medical people if they can do anything for her." She handed the girl off to one of the stockmen. "The rest of you – back to work!" She snarled the last in an uncharacteristic display of irritability.

The incident had brought up some very dark memories of the past. They were Myra's demons: demons she would probably fight the rest of her life. Myra returned to her office and sat motionless in her desk chair. Fellow employees filed by the office to check on her. They were worried by her recent change in demeanor. They worried if maybe they should have her checked out by the EMT's. No one was brave enough to approach her. She did not look in the mood for a chat.

Myra was lost in a sea of confusion and despair as she wrestled to overcome those dark feeling and emotions that she had brought back from the war. A tear formed in the corner of her eye. She began to shake. Her lips trembled.

Thirty minutes later, Myra emerged from her office cave. She walked the store as before, this time in quiet meditation. Employees scurried to their tasks making sure not to make eye contact. They did not want to upset her. They didn't know what to expect; she could snap at any moment.

Myra ended up at the front of the store. She paused at checkout number three. She spent a moment just looking. Then moving to the candy display, she picked out two of the lollipops. She tapped the mother in line on the back shoulder. "S'ok?" The mother nodded approval.

Seconds later, Myra had two new friends and IGA had two new future loyal customers, one six years old, the other four. Myra allowed a smile to form on her lips. Myra noticed Janey was back from the EMT's. She visited her station and hugged the girl, maybe a little longer than necessary.

IGA had their Assistant Manager back.

Falling

It's generally nicer to have. That's what Daniel K. Thorp believed. He preferred you call him Daniel, not any of that familiar Danny stuff. He was practiced introducing himself as Daniel K. Thorp, the K stands for 'charismatic', although it was widely thought he might not be as loaded with charm as he himself assumed. One thing was certain, though, he liked to have.

And he not just liked to have, he had to have. And not just had to have, he had to have the best. The best wine, the best wife, the best house, heck, even the best shoe shine. He surrounded himself with what he deemed were the best and he considered anyone who didn't have what he had to be a 'loser'. Life was one big game to him and he would win it. He would have.

Where this notion arose in his thinking was a cause for speculation. Some said that it stemmed from his father. His father had been a stern man with strict requirements for his approval. Daniel wanted nothing to do with philanthropy. He considered that weakness. Weakness in the donor as well as the donee.

Daniel was on his third marriage. He kept upgrading his mate when the former one aged past his liking. He had some children, more for the having of the kids, rather than the nurturing. He paid big money, however, for their upkeep at some of the best private boarding schools on the east coast. His wives cost a pretty penny, but, again, he liked having the best, and if that meant spending a little to get it, then so be it.

Daniel ran a construction concern is his little town. He was close in with all of the local politicians, donating to their reelection campaigns to curry their favor. It was no coincidence, then, that the DK Thorp Construction Company garnered virtually every public contract on which they bid.

Daniel was shrewd negotiator, having learned early on that one's profit at the end of a contract depended largely on the costs of construction. He cared not what quality of the materials he used to build his projects, as long as he could shave the costs down. He would routinely swap higher rated steel for lower grades. 'The engineers always design for worse case scenarios', was his mantra.

He had a reputation among the trades in the town that he was loathe to pay at times. If a job hadn't been executed to his extreme standard of quality, the subcontractor wouldn't be paid. He wanted the best after all. Even if the poor sub completed a flawless task, he would wait long periods to receive his payment. Daniel Thorp knew the time value of money and the longer he kept it, the more he would make. The result of these standard procedures of the Thorp Company left the tradesmen of the town reticent to work. That is, until they looked at the alternative: the Thorp Company controlled most of the jobs in town.

The town was building a new high-rise of low income housing, and to no one's surprise Thorp got the winning bid. Daniel was especially excited as he anticipated a very lucrative profit from this project. He arranged with the local news to hold a news conference where he could describe to the citizens all of the benefits and luxuries they would be building into the structure. Daniel knew the power of good press, and the politicians that he depended upon also benefitted from these self-laudatory, self-aggrandizing little spiels he pulled off from time to time.

The cameras focused on a podium, Daniel K Thorp strode to the microphone, having been introduced by the mayor. Thorp promised a building of soaring height with aesthetic architecture where the 'simple folk' as he described them could work and love and play. He furthered that everyone would be amazed at the quality of the structure, as the Thorp name was synonymous with excellence: the best.

A year passed and the 'Thorp Arms', as the building had become to be known colloquially, had risen high on the town's skyline. Every visitor to their environs was shown the structure with great pride. The town elders praised it as good governance. The media applauded with the rest. It was time for the unveiling.

Daniel K woke up early in the morning and donned his best imported Italian suit. He selected his most expensive tie, because expense was synonymous with the best. He called for his housemaid to bring the shoes she was supposed to be shining, and finding those of an acceptable but not perfectionary state, he shoved his bloated feet into them. He would need to buy some larger shoes eventually but today he needed to look good for the cameras.

Daniel had his driver bring the car around, and taking the elevator from his penthouse apartment, he crossed the lobby and got inside. He urged the man to drive fast, as he was running late, and in no time they arrived at the front courtyard of his newest building.

The media was already setup, and all of the most important people of the town had gathered to witness this historic dedication to government's effort to serve their community. The mayor was first on the list of speakers and droned seemingly incessantly. Daniel Thorp was about to drift off to sleep when he was announced to give his thoughts on the gravity of the occasion.

Daniel stepped to the microphone and gave an inspired speech about the benefits of public and private cooperation. He described in great detail the number of man-hours used to create the building. He praised the unspoken hordes of tradesmen needed to bring such a project to completion. Finally he finished with a dramatic pause as he pulled from behind the dais a metal box with a large bright green button on top.

"Ladies and gentlemen, I give you Thorp Arms!"

The audience erupted with applause and cheers. Daniel pushed down in exaggerated fashion on the green button and looking behind him waited with everyone in attendance at what the result of his action would be. He wouldn't have to wait long.

What followed was a chain of events that many of the workers on the project could probably have predicted, but those at the dedication did not. The green button was designed to electronically open the two large front doors that allowed access to the great lobby inside. The doors did open, but in so doing they slipped their tracks and flopped to the ground spraying glass shards in all directions.

There was a gasp as the crowd tried to make sense of what they had just seen. Before they could process the unfortunate breaking of the front doors, the masonry above the doors began to give way. Brick by brick the building's façade stripped away until there was a rather large pile of them obscuring the view of the lobby that the fallen doors had provided.

This eventuality triggered a mini riot in the onlookers. Politicians trampled their aides in an effort to find safety. The news reporters jumped in front of their cameras to not waste such a career defining event. A cloud of dust had formed that now enveloped the mob such that they could only hear what followed, not see exactly.

Daniel had negotiated with his concrete provider to use a weaker mix of concrete than was called for by the engineers. This was his usual method and had served him well in the past. What

Daniel had failed to recognize, however, was that this was the tallest building he had ever attempted. The strain of the weight of the extra floors had necessitated using the stronger concrete. The concrete provider had been so adamant about not using the weaker mix, he had made Daniel sign a waiver, indemnifying him from fault.

The building collapsed into itself, throwing debris for hundreds of yards. Everyone in the area ran about coughing and sneezing. Every respiration was being clogged by the mountain of dust that rained on the party. Daniel himself was covered white, his expensive Italian suit ruined.

That wasn't all that was ruined that day. The local politicians beat a hasty retreat from their erstwhile donor and supporter. The news was rife with folks falling over each other to denounce the criminal and immoral behavior of the Thorp Corporation. They vowed recompense.

Daniel himself had to hire a team of lawyers. He hired the best, because ... well you know. The lawyers kept the litigation churning for a full year before a verdict was delivered. Daniel K. Thorp was convicted of criminal negligence and sentenced to 10 years imprisonment. The civil suits brought against him ended in DK Thorp having to liquidate his company as well as all of his personal assets to pay the decisions. The court ordered liquidator got plenty of money for the assets; they were the best after all. It still wasn't enough to pay the entire bill. Fortunately for the lawyers, they had gotten their fees upfront.

Daniel was taken into custody and sent to prison. He would spend the next years in relative isolation. His trophy wife divorced him, and his kids actually didn't even know or care to what prison he had been sent.

Prison was hard for Daniel. He was used to having, and having the best. He had been reduced to living in a room six feet by ten feet that he shared with a large tattooed man named Duffy. Duffy was a very passionate man and gave Daniel the best of his love as often as he could. Daniel grew tired of getting the best from Duffy.

There was a subcontractor Daniel had used over the years in the same prison. He had turned to a life of robbery after the Thorp Company ruined his reputation in the business. He made sure to give Daniel his best each and every time he could find him. Daniel tired of his attentions.

In the end, Daniel still loved his life of having. He had had the best that a materialistic life could offer. He was a winner, not a loser like everyone he knew.

One night he fashioned a noose from twisting strips from his prison uniform. He admired his creation and gauged it the best and finest noose he had ever seen. He wanted to have the best. He needed to have the best for what would come next. He threw the makeshift rope lasso, with its twisted loop at the end, over the pipe in his and Duffy's room.

A Love Story

Edna Butterfield lay in state at Robertson's Funeral Home just north of the Cadillac dealership. She lay in a cherry wood coffin with a beautiful spray of roses and lilies adorning. A crowd of well-wishers were in attendance at her viewing. Her church group was there. The cousins and in-laws all made an appearance. The kids were there. Crissy, her youngest, was having the hardest time, just having lost her father days earlier.

A line started to form as the people queued up to pay their last respects. The onlookers commented on how well Edna looked. They marveled at the skill of the Robertsons: they had done a masterful job of presenting the corpse.

"Such a romance, Edna and Wilbur!" Edna's church group had gathered in the corner to commiserate. "She just couldn't bear to be apart from her dearest Wilbur." The ladies bowed their heads in memory of their friend. "Just three days since Wilbur died, and Edna passed to be with her love." They were in agreement.

↔

Three days earlier, Edna Butterfield sat in her dining room staring at her husband. There in the living room sat Wilbur in his underwear, playing solitaire on the coffee table while watching TV. He had blasted the volume of the TV to the max as he hadn't put in his hearing aids yet. Edna stewed in anger. The unmitigated boorish selfishness! How was she supposed to think?

And it wasn't just the volume of the TV. He didn't even have the decency to dress anymore. What if someone popped by for a visit? And by the way, she told herself, washing those bio hazardous underwear had been no picnic these 42 years!

But the thing that galled her above all others, the thing that was unforgiveable was the roast beef. She had labored in her garden all day the day before, with the only thing keeping her going was the thought of having that roast beef sandwich at the end of it. There had been one thick slice of that succulent rosy red roast she had pulled off on Sunday and she wanted nothing but it and some mayonnaise between two slices of bread. She thought of nothing else the whole day but diving into the culinary treat.

The sandwich was not to be, however. She entered the house at days end and noticing a dirty dish in the sink and immediately checked the refrigerator. The beef was gone! She seethed with hatred and loathing from that moment onward. The unmitigated selfishness!

Sitting in the dining room and, having nothing to do, as concentration with the loud TV was not to be, she perused the newspaper. There on page three was a story of a man who had accidentally shot himself while cleaning his gun. How in the world would someone do that, she mused. It seemed from the article that that kind of accident was fairly commonplace. Edna couldn't shake that last bit. It was almost expected, she figured.

She wasted no time and visited her laptop where she investigated the ways someone could accidentally shoot themselves while cleaning a gun. Her Wilbur had a pistol he kept in the bedroom in the table on his side of the bed. It would need to be cleaned from time to time to keep it in good working order. She read on and made several mental notes.

Confident in her plan, Edna marched upstairs to the bedroom to secure the gun. Checking the clip and snapping a round into the chamber she climbed down the stairs to the living room. Standing behind Wilbur, she placed the gun in an upturned angle under his chin and pulled the trigger. The spray of blood and brains on the ceiling told Edna that her plan not only was in action, it was going well.

She quickly clicked the magazine of bullets out of the gun and placed it on the table. She rushed to the basement where Wilbur kept his cleaning kit and, bringing that to the living room, laid the contents of the kit on the coffee table. All that was left was the frenzied call to 911 to get the police to witness her tragedy and get the body removed. That done, she proceeded to the kitchen where she would wash the gunpowder residue from her hands.

Wilbur's funeral had been a reflective crying fest where the lack of real gun control in this country had taken front row in the conversations of the attendees. Edna was in full form, wailing her lament that her one true love having been taken from her so tragically, and without warning. She bemoaned the unfairness of this sudden twist of fate.

After the interment, Wilbur's wake was well attended. The detective that had been assigned to the case was there. Edna knew she would have to produce her best performance here, to deflect any lingering doubt the detective might have as to the actual cause of the death. She pulled out all of the stops and, by the end of the day, her house was emptied of the mourners with no police in sight.

Edna smiled the smile of one released from prison after 42 years. There was a skip in her step. She hummed a little tune.

Edna made her way to the kitchen, where, way in the back of the cupboard, behind the cornmeal and flour, she found her secret stash. It was a bottle of Kalua liqueur, and she would fill a giant glass half full of it: the other half milk. She drank deep of the beverage, she needed it to calm the nerves of the day.

↔

Unbeknownst to Edna, Wilbur had gotten up early the day she had spent tending her garden. He had a list of errands to run. He searched the house for Edna, but she was nowhere to be found. 'Typical', he thought. He gathered his keys and his wallet and headed to the garage.

There in the yard was his Edna. She was busy ripping up the yard again, to what end he did not know. She was the most selfish woman he had ever known and why, oh why, he had spent 42 years with her was beyond him. She always had time for everyone else but him. He was the lowest priority on her priority list.

He paused to consider asking her if she needed anything while he was out, but decided not. He levered himself into his car and igniting the engine sped on his way. He wouldn't return until lunch time.

Back from his chores, which included a stop at the Wholesale club to pick up some salt for the water conditioner, Wilbur unloaded his plunder into the house and, having worked up a sweat, he lumbered to the kitchen.

Wilbur had been planning on a roast beef sandwich for lunch. He had placed a dish with the bloody section of delicious beef flesh in the back of the refrigerator so as to avoid the gaze of others. When he opened the door of the ice box, he found to no delight that his treasured luncheon would not be. The beef was gone.

That cut it. That woman knew no bounds of selfishness! It was bad enough that she clipped her toenails on his side of the bed, but now this? He would fix her, and fix her good! The utter gall in eating the last piece without as much as a how do you do!

Wilbur visited the garage to study his collection of household chemicals he stored there. There were bottles for weed control; bottles for fertilizing plants; bottles for killing insects. Those were all possibilities in his book, but his gaze had settled on a box in the corner. The box was old and faded. The lettering he could just make out, it was rat poison. He considered the label and being assured by the presence of strychnine in the concoction, he had his winner.

Into the kitchen he strode, rat poison under his arm. He walked up to the cupboard, the one that fooled no one, where the selfish shrew kept her hidden stash. Opening the Kalua bottle, he poured a very healthy dose of the poison. He poured until he was unsure if any more would change the taste or texture of the drink; then he stopped.

↔

Back in the kitchen, Edna was drinking deep form her stress reducing mixture of Kalua and milk. The combination reminded her of the chocolate milk of her youth, this time laced with that oh so sweet burn of the alcohol that would transport her to a land where care and woe had been banished. Edna didn't make it long after her drink. Not feeling well, she went to bed. She would never awaken.

↔

The visitation for Edna Butterfield was winding down. Just close friends and family were left. Crissy dried her eyes, she would have to go on without her parents. The children of Edna and Wilbur gathered in a group. Bobby, the first born son, spoke first.

"They were good parents, weren't they." The kids all agreed they were.

"The best!" Crissy wanted that known.

"Mom was always such a good cook." Second born Isaac spoke up. There was unanimous agreement.

"Funny story." Third born Henry always like to lighten the mood. "I stopped by to see them just days ago. Mom was in the yard doing something so I never saw her, and Dad was gone so I just put my feet up and waited. I was kinda hungry not having had any breakfast, I ransacked the 'frig. Guess what I found?"

The other kids were in rapt attention waiting to hear what he could have possibly found there.

"I found one of the biggest juiciest slices of Mom's famous roast beef!" Bobby rubbed his stomach in feigned demonstration of his jealousy.

"It was red and rosy just like Mom always used to make. So I made a sammich and ate! It was soooo good!" The group forgave this lapse of etiquette in their brother, not having saved any for them. They all lamented the fact they had not been there to, if not get the treat themselves, share in its succulence.

"Theirs was a love indeed. One that will not be seen anytime soon." Henry fixed his gaze skyward in contemplation of his parent's relationship. "A love to rival them all."

Catfish Supper

Jack poured a cup of coffee and admired his gear positioned by the door. He had laid the equipment out the night before, hoping to get an early start on his fishing. He knew a great place where the catfish grew big and fat. He would bag many of them before the day was over, he was sure. Today was his day. His excitement grew as his cup emptied.

There was a note on the kitchen table that caught his eye. His wife, Jamie, always went to bed later than he, and, as was her wont, she would from time to time leave him these little notes. This one stated:

"Air Conditioner broken again."

He sighed. He didn't know much about women, and he knew even less about menopausal women, but he knew that his wife was deeply invested in keeping the air conditioning going, especially in these sizzling days of July. He could dodge a lot of chores, he figured, but having retired from a 32 years HVAC career, this wasn't going to be one of them.

He plopped his coffee mug in the sink and headed to the garage. He kept his old tools in a cabinet by the garage window, and he pulled out the diagnostic devices he would need. He carried what he could to the compressor beside the house and, making several trips, he had his gear in place. A cursory check of the electronics assuaged his concerns for a burned computer board. He next investigated the high pressure components, and found with no surprise that he probably had a mal-functioning solenoid valve. How many of these he had replaced in his career was beyond his counting, but make no mistake about it, this compressor was never going to work without a new one.

He went back inside the house and washed his hands. He called up the stairs to Jamie that he was going to town to get a part. He grabbed his keys from the bowl in the hallway and jumped in his truck. He hadn't made it halfway to the hardware store when steam started to rise from the front hood.

Out he jumped from the driver position and, clicking the latch on the hood, waited for the steam to abate so he could assess which of the hoses had blown. While he was waiting, he perused the contents of the truck's bed to see if there was anything there that might help in making a temporary patch. He found some wire that had been left from the last project he had attempted. That would do nicely.

Back under the hood, he wrapped the blown hose in the wire. It wasn't a pretty fix, but it might suffice until he could get to Ed's Auto Shop in town. He slammed the hood shut and proceeded on his way.

Ed was a friend from church and he always threw his repair business his way. He pulled his truck into the second bay as Harvey, Ed's mechanic, was busy under a Buick in bay one. He pulled the truck over the lift rails and killed the engine. Steam was pouring from the semi-repaired hose he'd wired before. Harvey rolled out from under the Buick.

"Blown radiator hose, huh." He wiped his hands on a greasy rag.

"Yep. You think you guys got a new one for me?"

Harvey unlatched the truck hood and in seconds emerged confident of what was wrong. The mechanic thought for a minute and then walked over to an array of hoses they kept on the wall of the shop. He took a book from the end of the display and, thumbing through it, he stopped on the page listing the specifications for the pickup. "Less see…"

Jack waited eagerly to hear the prognosis for a successful repair. He wouldn't wait long.

"Well, we ain't got one of those right now."

Jack winced.

"But I think we can get it on today's delivery if we hurry." Harvey ambled into the office and dialed a number on the phone; one that he had memorized.

Harvey returned to Jack and gave him the news. "They'll have it here ASAP!"

Now Jack had dealt with Harvey before. ASAP didn't mean to Harvey what it meant to everybody else. Harvey thought of ASAP as maybe, 'As Soon as Pleasant' or 'At Slow Awkward Pace'. Jack had some time to kill and he knew it.

Jack moseyed out of the shop and eyeing May's Diner across the street, opted to have a look see. Inside the diner he recognized some old buddies. He occupied the seat they proffered.

The waitress was efficient, if not friendly. She pounced on Jack and inquired as to his culinary needs.

"Just coffee." Jack wasn't about to spoil his catfish dinner with some greasy diner fare.

The boys talked the usual nonsense that boys talk about when they get together. Joe Collins was in rare form and actually told a joke that Jack hadn't heard him tell before. Their lunches consumed, the men filtered out one by one and Jack not having a good reason to occupy the table alone, decide to leave as well.

Jack took a peek inside the Auto Shop and found his truck still silent in bay two. He decided to walk the two blocks down to the park. There, at the park, he located a bench somewhat secluded from the raft of workers eating their brown bag lunches. He settled into his little slice of park majesty and closed his eyes.

He day-dreamed a bit. After he had gutted and skinned the fish, he would make up a batch of his famous frying crust. He would use some flour mixed with an equal part of cornmeal. To that would come salt, pepper, with onion and garlic powders. He would finish the concoction with his secret ingredients: paprika and cayenne pepper.

He could almost smell the catfish frying in the corn oil. He always used a couple of spoons of pork lard in his corn oil when frying. It gave the crust a crisper crunch along with that delicious porkiness. He hadn't decided what would accompany his fish on the plate, but corn for sure, and maybe some hush puppies. He would wash it all down with a tall glass of sweet tea.

A Frisbee hit Jack while in his reverie, and jolted him to reality once more. He'd better check on the truck, he figured. He rose to his feet in classic old man fashion and made for Ed's.

As he made his way up town, he was delighted to see his pickup parked out in front of the car shop. He hailed Harvey from the office and minutes later the mechanic greeted him.

"Got her all fixed up."

Jack was all admiration. "Well I really do appreciate you getting that part here so fast." Harvey rang up Jack's bill and Jack was off and running again.

Jack was headed back downtown to the hardware store, when he saw a familiar face hitch hiking beside the road. It was Jenny Hawkins, the neighbor kid. He pulled up beside her.

"Hey Jenny! Where you going?"

Jenny looked happy to see him. "I'm tryin' to get to the cabin. Dad's gonna meet me there."

The Hawkins' had a cabin on the lake and they used it frequently in the summer. Jack didn't like the idea of young kid, let alone a girl, hitchhiking. Heck he didn't like anyone doing it; it was an invitation to all kinds of bad.

"Jump in. I'll run you up there."

Jenny hopped up onto the passenger seat and away they went. The lake was very close. The town was practically built around it. It wasn't long and they arrived.

Jenny jumped out and thanked Jack. Jack waited to make sure she was safe, and it was good he did that as Jenny found the cabin locked. Jack vacated his truck and tried his luck at the front door.

It seemed that no one was home. Jenny didn't want to travel back to town and insisted that she was fine. Her Dad would be there soon, she insisted. Jack didn't like it but he went around to the back of the house and found a window that had been nailed shut. A visit to his truck produced a hammer and, with the forked end of the tool, he managed to pry the window open. It was then just a matter of giving Jenny a leg up and she jumped inside.

Jenny waved goodbye to Jack as he pulled away. She would be OK, he reasoned.

Jack checked his phone. Jamie had texted him.

"Please get sugar from IGA."

It was just a small detour so Jack navigated the towns' back roads and arrived at the IGA. He stopped to ask his friend, Bob, where he could find the sugar, but instead got embroiled in a conversation about the tax the county had enacted. It was going to bankrupt the grocery business; Bob was sure of that.

Jack pried himself loose of Bob and his controversial stance on taxation. He located the bakery aisle and found a 4 lb bag of pure cane sugar. He paid for his purchase and then trotted for the pickup. It was getting late and he feared the hardware store might close.

He made it just in time. Arlen Davis was about to lock the doors when Jack rushed to gain access.

"All I need is a Solenoid valve, and I know where they are!" He promised alacrity. Arlen nodded agreement and allowed Jack to get the part.

Jack, relieved at getting the part at last, sped homeward. The sun was setting and he would have to work fast to keep the light. His fingers flew with the speed of a master exercising his prowess. It didn't take long and the solenoid was replaced and the coolant topped.

Jack restored his tools to their garage cabinet home, and, entering the house, found proof of his skill in a cool breeze wafting over his overheated body. He washed his hands in the sink and then turned to the refrigerator.

Inside the ice box, he found another of Jamie's notes.

"Gone to church bake sale."

He was a little peeved that he had had to go out of his way to get the sugar, yet she had obviously found another source. Oh well, he searched for what she might have left.

Inside the ice cold cabinet, he found two wilted carrots, some green onions and a box of baking soda. There was a bowl of something that looked like tapioca, but smelled of mushrooms and had little green flecks inside. He decided to forgo all of those and take the single plastic wrapped slice of American cheese food-like product in the back.

He ate his cheese in silence, looking over at his fishing gear still standing guard by the door. He didn't get his catfish supper but just wait until tomorrow, he vowed. He would have the biggest, fattest catfish in the county on his plate! "Oh wait!" He thought. Tomorrow was his Shriner's meeting.

Rube Tribute

The house was filled with them. The garage was filled also. The backyard had very little grass growing, for all of the junk stored there. He would have filled the attic too, except for the piles of boxes his wife had stored there.

Denny Sparks was a Rube Goldberg machine fan. For those unfamiliar with the legacy of Rube, he was the father of a number of engineering competitions where the contestants vie to produce the most elaborate contraption possible that does absolutely little to no valuable work. The Rube Goldberg tradition is the basis for the board game, 'Mouse Trap'.

And so, Denny loved building his machines. He cruised the local junk yards weekly to see if any new junque had been deposited that might lend itself to Rube'ing. He piled the mostly metallic pieces in the backyard, where they waited to be used. If asked, Denny would tell you his wealth lay beyond, to the back of the house.

Denny's wife, Darla, was not such a Rube-ite. She was constantly complaining about the mess in the house. She hadn't been able to park her car in the garage for 10 years. Darla was fed up with all of the contraptions lying here and there. She viewed them with disgust.

"Why do we have to have all of these thing-a-ma-bobs taking up all of the useable space of our house?" She knew she was talking to the wall mostly; Denny was past listening to her concerns about his mechanical 'children'. "How am I ever going to be able to have any friends over with all of this mess, everywhere! I don't know how you can be so cruel!" Darla hated the machines with such a passion that, if she had possessed the power of telekinesis, she would have long ago converted the piles of metal and plastic to vapor.

Denny had to admit that he did take up a lot of the space, but he viewed it as engineering art of a kind. Darla should be proud of his achievements, he thought. He would have to clean some of it up, though. She was entitled to her spaces too, he owned.

Denny was working on his largest machine yet. It incorporated sixteen sub machines, linked together in exciting ways. He would complete this one, then move it to the already full garage. That was the plan. Just a couple of more tweaks here and there and his masterwork would be done.

The evening fell on their little chaotic domestic scene. Darla was in the kitchen putting away the remains of dinner. Denny was in the living room sipping a cup of tea and eyeing his creation. He was flummoxed as to how to complete the series of contraptions. The idea would come, he had no doubt. It would just take some cogitation.

A knock on the door woke Denny from his trance. He slowly righted himself from the easy chair that had been his place of repose, and opened his front door. A rather large redheaded man with a long beard pushed past him and entered the house uninvited. Denny thought this behavior quite inexcusable and voiced his disagreement.

"Hey!"

The red bearded man pulled a pistol from his coat pocket and shoved it in Denny's face. "You alone!?"

Denny had really never had a gun pointed at him before, and certainly not in such a violent threatening way. He tried to calm himself, and could only get out, "My wife..."

The house invader looked where Denny had been looking and noticed a yellow apron flying around the kitchen, purporting to have a lady dressed inside. The man indicated Denny' direction of walk, and the pair entered the kitchen.

"Oh my!" Darla dropped the dishes she was carrying. The shards of ceramic tinkled as they hit the tile floor and shattered.

The bearded felon was in no mood for dramatics. "Where's the money and the jewelry!?" He shoved his pistol deep into Denny's ribs.

Denny winced with pain. "The bedroom."

The man rounded up his captives and the trio made their way to the master bedroom. There the man directed while the husband and wife rounded up their entire life's cache of jewelry and the approximate two hundred dollars of cash on hand. The man pushed some of the furniture over, ostensibly looking for a safe or other. Satisfied that all of the loot had been gotten, the group made their way back to the living room.

The bearded man tossed a roll of duct tape to Darla. "Tape him to that chair." He pointed to one of the hard wooden chairs in the room. Darla pushed the chair toward Denny.

The man suddenly became interested in the collection of metal structures arrayed across the room. "What's this thing?" He had a confused look on his face.

Denny knew he had a chance to educate this fellow in what was his life's passion. He gave his usual canned spiel about the history of the Rube Goldberg machine, except he shortened it quite severely as he didn't know how long this guy would keep his interest.

He asked the man if he would like to see it run. The man looked at the machine for a long time. The complexities of the apparatus both confused and marveled the robber. Finally after his long contemplation, he acceded by giving a slight nod to the affirmative.

Denny looked on the floor of the room for a white dot he had painted there. He turned to the man and indicated that he should step back a pace to the dot. "If you hold out your hand you can catch the candy."

Denny next positioned himself at the beginning of the contrivance, and pushing a lever, declared, "This is how you start it going."

The man stared in awe. The lever pushed a billiard ball that got rolling down a river of metal rods until it hit a catch at the bottom. The catch activated a small electric motor that pulled a string that pulled a latch from in front of a toy car high by the ceiling. The car obeyed gravity and drove onward.

The bearded man quietly chuckled at the whimsy. 'All of that just too get a car rolling!' He watched on like a child before a Christmas tree.

The car hit a dead end that sent a pretend air balloon flying across the room. The bearded man was laughing out loud now as the display was quite thrilling. Feature after feature of the machine revealed itself in a spectacle of the dramatic: a presentation unlike any he had ever beheld.

The machine was nearing the end of its series. The domino ladder had started Denny's homage to the Price Is Right with its climbing mountain climber. He had even taped a short yodeling track to play while the man climbed. It was an unrivalled feat of Rube-nificence.

The last maneuver followed the mountain climber. The bearded man held his un-gunned hand out farther. He didn't want to miss the candy. The climber triggered a device on the shelf above the bearded candy receptacle. The man looked up in rapt anticipation. He wouldn't have to wait long for his treat. Off the end of the shelf a sixteen pound bowling ball fell and hit Denny and Darla's uninvited guest squarely on the forehead. The man collapsed to the floor.

Denny got busy duct taping the new fan of his work. Darla called 911. The police arrived shortly and took the now reviving burglar into custody.

A week later, a group of women got together to taste some tea and gossip de la maison. Denny's wife was there and in rare form. She was all a dither, telling the girls of their brush with death. She told about dropping the dishes. The girls grimaced when she spoke of the gun in Denny's ribs. The part about the machine had the women laughing.

Denny walked into the living room, having gotten the part he needed from the back yard. "Good afternoon ladies."

The ladies paused in their conversations to acknowledge the ersatz engineer.

Darla was the first to speak. "Show them how it works!" The other ladies shrieked with anticipatory glee. "And then I want you to show them the one with the monkey that uses the cymbals!"

She turned to the woman next to her and whispered. "That's my favorite one."

How the Cow Ate the Cabbage

Two men sat in quiet repose under a sprawling chestnut tree. They lounged in comfort, allowing the rigors of the day to pass by unnoticed. The one man turned to his friend and asked, "You ever heard how the cow ate the cabbage?" His friend lifted his eyes to the heavens and contemplated. He slowly shook his head in the negative. His companion then sighed and, after composing himself for the telling, started his narration.

"The heat of the day had risen to its zenith. He had spent the morning mending the fence on his small farm when he noticed it out of the corner of his eye. He decided to take a rest from his labors and sit under the large oak at the edge of his property to, first, cool off a bit and, second, to witness the proceedings.

"What lay before him in the pasture was a rather large cow eyeing a rather large round vegetable lying in the grass. It was a large cabbage. How the cabbage had managed to make its way from his wife's garden to this place in the pasture was a mystery. But there the cabbage sat, and there the cow eyed it with ever increasing interest.

"He watched as the hungry bovine addressed the problem of eating the vegetarian spheroid. She nudged the flower of the brassica genus, hoping to get a clue how she would proceed. The nudging served two purposes. First, she could smell the treat to gauge its freshness. Rotten food, while still digestible, was not going to be of interest. The second benefit of her probing was to determine which face of the vegetable to attack.

"She decided the root end was the hardest part to tackle, but if she could crack that end, the rest would be easier. Turning the cabbage over with her nose, she clamped her incisors on the protruding root and, with a swift and mighty chomp, severed the root from the leafy head.

"A time of chewing ensued. The root was particularly fibrous and mastication of the food proved more difficult for her than previously evaluated. A trip to and from her fore stomach allowed the cow some much needed rumination: in the contents of her stomach as well as her place in the universe.

"Satisfied that the root had had been sufficiently broken down for easy digestion, she turned her attention to the head of the plant. Not having the root attached, the head had lost some of its structural integrity, but still the leaves hung together. She decided to start with the outer leaves as they seemed to be attached with less security.

"The leaves entered her mouth one by one and fell victim to the same fate as the root. Back and forth to the stomachs of the cow, they travelled a road of teeth, spittle and digestive juices. The brown, four legged enemy of all the cruciferous vegetation lowed a melody of satisfaction, as the sweet pasture treat shrunk in size with every bite.

"Finally, the cabbage was lost from sight. All that was left were small shards of the plant that had fallen from the cow's mouth to the grass on the surface of the earth below. The cow searched in apparent futility for any remains that could be gobbled. At last, before giving up, she found one lone leaf that had fallen from the globe early on in the process. She gleefully slurped the loner up and swallowed it to join its brothers.

"Finished with the cabbage, the cow turned to leave the area. She searched for other more favorable venues where other delicacies may be found. As she waddled away, the farmer was rewarded for his attention. She, wanting to complete her alimentation, left a hot steaming pile of processed roughage for his examination."

The man fell back to where he was laying before, somewhat exhausted for the telling. His friend quietly judged the story he had just heard. The man rolled over to rest his elbow on the ground and his head in the palm of his hand. His eyes squinted with a profound display of confusion. He opened his mouth to speak, but no words would come.

Finally in a desperate attempt to coalesce his thoughts and gain closure of his interpretation of the story, the man gasped. "That's the stupidest thing I've ever heard."

Wilted Flowers

The soup simmered nicely on the small gas stove. The odor of roasted mushrooms and garlic filled the kitchen. The old man stirred his lunch with a long wooden spoon. Happy that his concoction was ready for consumption, he sprinkled some chopped parsley on top of the brew and shut the fire off underneath.

A visit to the cupboard produced a bowl and a saucer. The bowl was for him; the saucer for his cat, Hardy. He pulled a large soup spoon from the drawer by the sink and, stopping by the refrigerator, he gathered a small carton of cream. Juggling the dishes and cream in his arms, he laid the equipment for his luncheon on the kitchen table and ladled a heaping serving of his soup into the bowl. Hardy liked to eat with him, so he poured a deep pool of cream into her saucer, with a little dollop of the cream for his soup.

Hardy purred as she lapped up the creamy liquid. The old man sighed in delight at the heavenly delectability of his concoction. He grabbed a small vase on the table and gave it a more prominent situation. He smiled at the flowers. They were wilted with age but to him they still held a deep abiding beauty.

He had rescued the flowers from his dear wife's funeral. They had been married how many years and, even after this time, he still missed her. All the good things in his life had come from this sweet little girl, with whom he had built a life.

Lunch over, he blew the flowers a kiss and got to the task of cleaning up. Today was his errand day. He had some groceries to buy and some checks to deposit at the bank. He gave Hardy a vigorous back rub and rummaged in the hall closet for a jacket.

His bank was just down the road beside the mini mall. He pulled into an empty spot by the ATM machine and ventured into the neighborhood money repository. The lobby of the bank was virtually empty. Most people did their banking online, but he had never trusted that. He assumed there were all kinds of devious people just waiting outside his house to capture his password and steal his meager life savings.

His favorite teller was open, so the old man found a home at her window.

"Hello Mr. Walker." The girl gave the man a knowing smile. She liked the old guy. He was always giving her some kind of pretend grief.

"Hello Sheila. I've got a major financial transaction to do today." The man winked.

Charlie Walker gave the girl his checks and waited as Sheila the teller processed the documents with competent alacrity and precision. Having finished the tasks, the young lady asked, "Anything else today?"

Old Mr. Walker thought for a moment and answered, "Oh, I need some cash."

The teller smiled knowing something was coming. "How much shall I put you down for?"

"Well I've got to get the yacht remodeled, and then there's the pool I'm putting in at the house in Monaco…" The old guy winked again. "I guess $60 will do…"

Sheila counted out the gentle man's cash and was about to wish him a pleasant day, when four men wearing Halloween masks entered the bank lobby.

The largest of the four fired a gun in the air. The bullets hit the ceiling and caused a rain of plaster dust. "Everyone freeze and step away from the counters!"

Before anyone could assimilate what was actually happening, one of the four jumped behind the counter into the teller's area and another two of them pulled the bank manager and his assistant out into the lobby.

The large man held out a bag and demanded everyone to put in their phone. "Everyone remain calm and no one gets hurt!" The large man seemed to be the one in charge.

The men proceeded to get the contents of the teller's drawers, minus the dye packs. The two with the managers forced their way into the safe and made quick time of relieving the bank of all things valuable found there. Reassembled in the lobby, the four turned to leave. The large robber grabbed Sheila by the hair. "You're coming with us!"

Sheila shrieked with horror. She absolutely did not want to go with the men. There was no telling how that would end. She struggled underneath the pulling and tugging the large man wielded to make her comply.

"Take me instead." The old man stepped up to the large man and put his hand on the man's shoulder. "She's scared and unpredictable. I'm very cooperative."

The large man's initial reaction was one of violence. He shook the old man's hand from his shoulder and turning to him shoved his pistol into the old man's cheek. "So you want to be the hero, huh!?"

"Yes." The old man didn't know how to respond to that, but he didn't want his friend to leave with the men. He had had his life. She hadn't even started hers.

The felon considered the old guy. "OK tough guy, let's go!" The large man shoved him in the back to get him going.

Outside of the bank, a cargo van was waiting. The men threw the old man into the back and immediately started duct taping his arms and legs. They slipped a cloth bag over his head, and filled his mouth with a dirty cloth rag that they proceeded to duct tape to his face.

The group drove in silence. Minutes later, the muted sounds of police sirens could be heard. Those were met with sounds of laughter from the robbers. The old man waited in silence, wondering what fate the gang had in mind for him. He wouldn't wait long.

The van pulled to a stop. The men jumped out and began the task of offloading their booty. The old man couldn't tell exactly, but he thought he heard the sound of a trunk opening. They must be changing vehicles, he surmised.

Moments later, the large one grabbed him by his jacket collar and pulled him out of the van. "Sit here!" The man unceremoniously plopped the aging man in a hard metal chair. The robber then pulled out more duct tape and commenced taping the already incapacitated man to the metal chair.

The old man was ready. He knew it was possible they wouldn't want to leave him alive to tip off the police, but he also wondered how stupid you'd have to be to add murder to your bank robbery and kidnapping. Killing him would bring too much focus on them. It turned out the old man was right. After some shuffling around, the group of criminals jumped into their new car and, shutting the doors, sped off.

The old man waited to make sure they actually were gone. He could smell plastic burning, and hear the roar of some flames. He assumed they had torched their getaway van. The heat from the fire grew and he felt the scorching sensation on his face. He jumped with every tire that exploded.

He was feeling discomfort from the binding on his hands, so he started working there first to see if he could loosen the tape. They had woven the tape tightly, and so his progress was slow.

Eventually, he was able to free one hand from the tape. One hand free was all he needed. He made quick work of the other encumbrances. When he had the cloth bag removed from his head, he found he was sitting square in the middle of an abandoned warehouse. The charred remains of the getaway van was smoldering in the corner of the expansive, rusting building.

He made his way from the warehouse to the street. He spied a gas station down the highway and made his way there. Inside the gas station he borrowed the phone and called the police.

The next morning, he was up at the usual time. Hardy didn't allow him to sleep in; she wanted what she wanted, when she wanted. The old man had spent so much time with the police the day before, he had totally forgotten to go to the grocery. The pantry was fairly bare, so he decided to forego breakfast.

Hardy was on the table, in position. He brought over a small bowl of cat food. She wanted more cream, he knew, but she would get cat food. She ate her breakfast, purring in satisfaction.

He had underestimated his chances of less excitement for the day. A knock came to the front door. He ambled to the door and answered. Outside, on his porch, was a young lady with a microphone and a cameraman, ostensibly with a running camera as the light fixture on top of the camera was fully ablaze.

Supposedly, the news of his abduction had hit the newsrooms in town and they all wanted an interview. The old man acceded to their requests. He really didn't feel like the hero they were claiming him to be. He had acted out of logic mainly.

The news painted him with a rather heroic brush. One reporter had questioned his sanity/intelligence in volunteering for the abduction. The old man chuckled. "Maybe that guy is onto something."

It was time to start his chores anew. He put on his jacket and made his way to the grocery. His visit there took longer than expected. He was stopped numerous times by well-wishers and selfie paparazzi. At the checkout line, the store manager intervened and told him his groceries were 'on the house'.

He hated all of the fuss. He enjoyed his quiet, if a bit lonesome, life. He was not ready, however, for what he found when he pulled into his driveway.

His porch was full of flowers, balloons and cards: more well-wishers. He put his groceries away, then started the task of moving the bounty of flowers and balloons inside the house. When completed, his house smelled of flowery perfume. "Not unlike a New Orleans whore house", he mused.

Lunchtime had come, and he was hungry from his morning labors. He quickly heated his soup from the day before and, pouring a small dish of cream for Hardy, the pair sat down for their meal.

The old man sat there looking at the array of colorful flowers he had placed on the kitchen table. A large vase full of roses, irises and wild flowers filled his view. They were beautiful. He slowly pushed them aside to reveal his wilted flowers. He pulled those to the front so he could see them better. The old man ate his soup in silence, Harpy stuck her nose in his bowl looking for more cream.

He loved the colorless, odorless wilted flowers. They were the prettiest, after all.

The Mayonnaise Apocalypse

Colonel Marcus Cornelius Higginbottom ran a tight ship. Well, actually, it wasn't a ship at all, but a small base of the US Army. A base that was landlocked. In the middle of the country. Except for that creek that ran by the base about a mile or two up the road.

So as it was, Colonel Higginbottom ruled with an iron fist. Actually, his fist was made of flesh like the rest of us. He hadn't actually struck anyone in anger since that ruckus with the guy hitting on his girlfriend in high school. Funny, he couldn't remember the boy's name. He deserved it, though.

Let's just agree that Colonel Marcus Higginbottom had a lot of rules. And like most army base commanders, he expected his rules to be followed. He gave his orders and left the implementation of those orders to his men under him. He was proud of his men.

And so, it was with some degree of trepidation that the Colonel invited the mess cook, Sargent Grimes into his office.

"Sargent Grimes, sir!" Grimes snapped to attention.

The Colonel finished reading the report on his desk and slowly folded the manila folder that contained it, to a close. "At ease." The Colonel reached for his coffee mug and reclined in his office chair. "What can I do for you Sargent?"

"We've got a bit of a problem, sir." The Sargent seemed nervous. What would follow would not please his commander.

"Well out with it soldier! What's this disaster that merits you disturbing my morning cup?"

"We're out of mayonnaise, sir."

The Colonel almost laughed out loud, the problem seemed ridiculous. The Sargent knew better, though. The Colonel insisted on mayonnaise for his July 4th burger.

The Colonel grew up in the Midwest of the country where his family always celebrated the fourth of July with a BBQ of some sort. And that BBQ always included grilled hamburgers, upon which the Colonel always put a rather large slather of mayonnaise. Their tradition was a red, white and blue burger. The tomato was the red, the mayo was the white and the crushed blue corn chips they sprinkled on top was the blue. Beyond that, Colonel Higginbottom considered mayonnaise the only way a real American would eat a burger. And rest assured, they would have burgers on the fourth!

"No mayo you say…" The Colonel took a large slug of his coffee. "Now, Sargent, how are we going to have our Fourth of July without mayonnaise?"

"That's just it, sir. We've run out. And begging your pardon, sir, but it seems every grocery in the county has run out as well."

"Malarkey! How can every grocery run out of something so important the day before the big holiday?" He paused to think. "Dawson, in here now!"

Corporal Dawson flew into the office and snapped to attention. "At ease, corporal. I want you to get on the phone to every grocery in the area and find us some mayo."

"Mayo sir?"

"Yes, MAYO dammit!! Get moving!" The corporal flew out of the office.

"Now you ,Sargent."

"Yes, sir."

"How in the hell did you ever let us get in this predicament?"

"Well, sir, our delivery today was supposed…"

"I don't want excuses! Get out there and find us some mayo or by George Armstrong Custer you'll be a corporal by morning!" The colonel was on his feet now. "Dismissed!"

Grimes exited the office, visibly agitated.

The Colonel went on with his morning schedule, confident in his men. They would find the missing condiment if any could be found. It wasn't until lunch that he got the report.

"I sent my men out to scour the area, sir. All they found was this." Sargent Grimes held out an 8 ounce jar of Miracle Whiz.

"What the hell is this?" The colonel was unimpressed.

"Miracle Whiz, sir. Some folks say it tastes just like mayo."

"They do, do they Sargent?" The Colonel gave the Sargent a look like he had better judge his words very carefully in the next sentence.

"I'll keep looking, sir."

"You better damn do that."

The report from his office aide, Corporal Dawson, yielded less that satisfactory results. The Colonel reluctantly admitted that he would have to take matters into his own hands. If his men could put their lives on the line for God and country, then they deserved to get some doggone mayonnaise for their BBQ.

"It seems Kroft Foods made a run of mayo just yesterday, but they failed to deliver any of it. Unfortunately, the factory is closed down for the holiday." The corporal offered a ray of hope. Kroft was synonymous with the best mayonnaise money could buy. That, and apple butter.

That information was all the Colonel needed. "Get me Lieutenant Wilson!"

He wouldn't wait long. Wilson strode into his office and snapped to attention.

"At ease."

"You sent for me, sir?"

"Wilson, I have a mission for you. Actually a mission for us."

"For us, sir?"

"Yes. I want you to assemble a team of six of your best men and meet me in 30 in the briefing room."

"Yes, sir. Begging you pardon, sir. What kind of mission is it? What kind of skills do we need?"

"We need muscle. We need electronic surveillance expertise. We need a helicopter."

"Right away, Colonel!" The Lieutenant made haste to his tasks. He had wanted some real world experience, and it seemed like he would finally be getting some.

Thirty minutes passed, and the Colonel set his feet into the briefing room to find his team already assembled, and eagerly awaiting the details of their mission. The Colonel strode to the dais and started the briefing.

"Men, we are on a mission to get mayonnaise for our company picnic tomorrow."

The men looked at each other in disbelief. 'Mayonnaise?' was the question of everyone's mind. Did they hear that right?

"That's right, sweet, creamy, luxurious mayo." The Colonel raised his eyes skyward in blissful remembrance of the sandwiches he had enjoyed. He continued. "There's a Kroft factory not 30 clicks from here with a warehouse full of mayo. They made the stuff but the idiots forgot to deliver it, I guess."

The Colonel went on to outline his plan of attack. The men sat in rapt attention. They knew the commander would be accompanying them and they had no wish to disappoint him. When all were agreed on the details, and who had what responsibility, the men began suiting up for the task.

"Wilson." The Colonel called the lieutenant over. "I want only rubber bullets on this. We don't want any accidental civilian casualties." Wilson nodded agreement. "We go at zero dark hundred."

"Yes, sir." The lieutenant gathered his men and gave the instructions.

Midnight clicked over a new day on the clock and the team boarded their Blackhawk helicopter. The ride to the factory would be short. The men spent their time checking their ammo and adjusting their night vision goggles.

The parking lot behind the factory seemed like the perfect assault point. The pilot gently laid the copter shoes on the asphalt. The men inside hit the ground at a run. They broke off into groups, the Colonel barking orders as they moved.

Corporal Stevens was responsible for the alarm systems and so made his way to the roof. His intel had given the roof as the likely point of attack for neutralization. Private Holmes was in charge of killing the power to the giant warehouse. He followed the point men to the back door of the building.

The radio communication system they were using crackled. "Alpha team in place." The soldiers by the back door were ready.

"Just a second." Stevens hadn't broken the alarm system yet. And then, "Alarm is a go."

"Alpha you are a go." The Colonel watched as his troops pried the back door open with an oversized crowbar.

Once inside, Alpha team had two responsibilities. Holmes would seek out the power, while the other two looked for possible night guards or any other possible problems. It wasn't long and the warehouse fell in darkness. The men pulled their night vision equipment over their heads.

Sargent Cummins and Private Ernst were the Omega team. They were responsible for the retrieval of the mayonnaise. They entered the darkened warehouse and began a systematic search of the premises.

"Hold." Alpha team had spotted something. "Guard. Northside. Pursuing now." The men quickly flanked the flashlight carrying keeper of the Kroft Foods treasure. Once the guard was within striking range, the soldiers pounced and subdued the aging erstwhile centurion.

"Where is the mayonnaise?" The soldiers snapped at the guard.

"Back dock." The old man had no intention of giving his life for a batch of whipped condiment.

"Guard subdued. Target substance on back dock." Alpha team tied the guard with zip ties and duct taped him to a chair in the break room.

Omega team sprinted to the dock and on arrival beheld an array of wooden pallets stacked full with cardboard boxes of mayonnaisey goodness. The men went to work cutting the plastic sheeting that held the boxes in place. The scooped up four cases of the ooey gooey silken treat and beat a retreat to the helicopter, but not before placing two one hundred dollar bills where the boxes used to be. The Colonel insisted on that.

"We have the prize." Omega team's announcement over the headsets met with hearty 'ooo-rahs' all around.

Alpha team was almost to the copter with Omega out of the back door when a police car pulled into the back parking lot. Two officers jumped out of the police cruiser and pulled their weapons. "Halt!"

The army soldiers reacted in instinctual fashion. No thought was needed. The men rained down a maelstrom of fire on the poor patrolmen. The police offered a bullet or two every so often, when the soldiers paused to reload, but it was obvious they were outgunned.

"I'm hit!" One of the policemen grabbed his head. He had taken a rubber bullet to the forehead.

"Where are you hit?" His partner ran to his assistance.

"Here." The man pulled his hand from his forehead expecting to see it washed with his own blood. Instead, his hand came back clean. "Huh?"

"You ain't hit!" His partner was annoyed.

"Look!" The officer with a welt growing larger and larger on his forehead pointed to the warehouse wall behind them. There, on the wall, could be seen an ocean of rubber bullets making small dents in the wall and falling to the ground. One bullet rolled to the officer. "Rubber!" The police were confused.

Lieutenant Wilson had watched the fire fight between the police and his men with extreme agitation. The police were using live ammo. He decided to give Omega team some cover, and so he stepped behind the mini Gatling gun installed on the Blackhawk and lay down a river of bullets straight into the policemen's patrol car. The effect was immediate destruction of the car. It would never be driven again.

The Colonel was aghast at this development. He grabbed Wilson by the arm and pulled. This action resulted in the Gatling gun now being aimed at a Maple tree that lined the lot. The gun made splinters of the tree's trunk in no time and, the structure of three being so degraded, the tree fell, laying a distinct barrier between the soldiers and the police. Their safety secured, the helicopter took off: all teams accounted for.

The ride back to base was jubilant. They hadn't planned on the police. They had persevered, though, in the greatest of Army tradition.

The Colonel noticed Ernst's arm was bleeding. "What's that Private?"

"Just a scratch, sir."

The Colonel pulled a bandage from his kit and wrapped the soldiers wound. He would recommend him for a Purple Heart.

Confident in their completed mission, the group then lay in silence, trying to come down from the excitement. The Colonel inspected their booty.

The first carton he examined had the Kroft logo as expected, but there was a picture of a young girl picking apples from an apple tree. That was curious to the Colonel, so he extracted the knife from his belt and opened the container. Inside he found jar upon jar of apple butter.

"Apple Butter!?" The Colonel was not pleased.

Feverishly, he opened the other three cartons only to be disappointed every time. In their haste, Omega team had picked up apple butter cartons, not mayonnaise. Omega team moved to sit in the back of the copter. They didn't want to hear anything the Colonel might say next.

The next day dawned upon a grateful nation celebrating their independence from Britain. The Colonel was up and running early to make sure all of the preparations for the day were in order. The base was being visited by Senator Bayles, so everything needed to be in ship shape. That is as ship shape as possible in a landlocked army base.

The Senator arrived, and the parades and inspections over, they settled down to their annual BBQ feast. There on the tables the cooks had arrayed all kinds of charred meats, chief among them, the hamburgers.

The Colonel picked up a plate and helped himself to a burger. There were his normal tomato slices and blue corn tortilla chips. He loved the idea of his red, white and blue burger. Red tomato, white mayo and blue corn chips. It was the tradition. Today that was not to be.

There on the table sat jars of the apple butter that signified their failure of the night before. Sighing noticeably, the Colonel slathered on the sweet cinnamon apply condiment on his burger bun. He then plopped on the burger, tomato and corn chips. He made his way to his seat beside the Senator.

He smiled and nodded to the dignitaries assembled, but his heart wasn't in it. He raised his burger to his mouth and ate. He was surprised at the result. He had expected a nauseating sensation, but he actually felt like he might actually like the combination of the apples and burger.

Senator Bayles leaned over to the Colonel. "My, what tasty burgers! Whose idea was the apple butter, if I might ask?"

The Colonel was surprised at this development. "Why I recommended it to the cook myself." The Colonel didn't get where he was by not taking credit when it was offered.

"Spectacular!" The Senator had never tasted such a treat.

"I thought it might signify our dedication to diversity, Senator. You know, we aren't all red, WHITE and blue. Some of the best of us are men of color."

The Senator laughed. "How true!"

He took another bite of the unanticipated gastronomic delight. He had to admit it, America never tasted so good.

Spirit Animal

A small lemon yellow bird rested on the left index finger of a man sitting on an office chair in his cubicle. The man stroked the little guy softly with the index finger of his right hand, smoothing the feathers from the head to the tail. The bird tweeted a heavenly melody in response. The man cooed his pleasure to his bird friend. "That's a good boy."

Outside the cubicle a small gathering of co-workers assembled. They watched incredulously as the man mimed stroking the feathers of an invisible companion. They could neither see nor hear the little bird.

"Hey BB, what you got there!?" The group roared with laughter. The man had been given the nickname 'Bird Brain' by his fellows, which had quickly been shortened to 'BB'.

"Can we fry up your bird for lunch?" Another round of giggles ensued.

Cole Palmer was used to this abuse. Actually, he was less used to it, as resigned to it. He loved his little canary friend. He named him Roy, and the bird was his best friend in the whole world. There were some days that he thought maybe only he and Roy existed on the planet. That everyone else was of a different species.

Cole often marveled why others couldn't see his little friend. Roy was a bright yellow. His song echoed through any room as a powerful sound. Roy filled Cole's heart with so much joy and delight, that Cole wondered sometimes if his heart would explode.

WINSTON ROBERTS

Roy and Cole worked on day after day, toiling in virtual isolation. Cole found it hard to relate to his comrades at the firm. Most just thought of him as crazy. Others were outright hostile in their bullying.

Roy wasn't faring well under the pressure. Every day his song became softer, less melodious, if that could even be. His feathers began to fall out. Cole was worried about his friend, that he might have contracted some kind of illness.

Cole took his buddy to a veterinarian. Back in an examination room, the trio inspected Roy to see what could be done.

"Umhmmm…" The doctor pulled out an examination light and inspected the bird. "It looks like he might need a change of diet."

Cole regarded the doctor with an aversive eye. What the doctor was examining was his examination table. Roy had flown onto his shoulder.

"I think we have just what you need." The doctor showed him the way to the checkout counter. He instructed his assistant to ring up a bag of their birdseed, as a prescription for the ailing avian.

Cole knew the doctor was just upselling him, but he needed some birdfeed anyway, and maybe this stuff would help. He was at his wit's end to help his friend.

The days that followed found Roy falling deeper and deeper into illness, as the ribbing Cole was getting at work increased. There were days when Cole would have an audience of six or more. Someone even printed out a banner for the front of his cubicle that they pinned under his name plate. It read:

"If it looks like a duck, and quacks like a duck, it must be crazy."

Cole immediately ripped the offending banner from its place of prominent display.

Roy was at a point now, that he spent most of the day in Cole's coat pocket, only coming out from time to time for fresh air. Roy's eyes had started to look hollow and depressed. Roy's feathers were paler now: less bright yellow, more dirty white. More and more feathers were falling too, leaving Roy with the look of having the mange or some other nasty infestation.

Eventually, Cole was surprised by a visit from the big boss. "Cole, I wonder if we could have a word."

Cole was suspicious of this attention. The big boss almost never came down to his area. "Sure."

Cole followed his employer to his office and the boss shut the door behind them.

"Cole. We have a problem."

Cole didn't like the tone of that. "We do?"

"It seems you and your bird are causing a disturbance in our little workplace."

"I can explain."

"No need. I have a difficult decision to make and what I've decided is … that you should find another place of employment."

"Is it my work?"

"No son, your work has been excellent."

"But I've done nothing wrong?"

"Well that may be so, but I can either let you go, or everyone else in the office. You tend to creep them out, Cole."

Cole had no words to combat that. He knew he wasn't like his co-workers, but he didn't think that required him being fired. He rose from his chair and headed back to his cubicle to get this things.

Security was waiting for him at his cubicle. They had been called to escort him from the building. Cole made sure Roy was safe and warm in his coat pocket, and piled some personal mementos he had displayed around his space, into a cardboard box that security had thankfully supplied.

The guards walked Cole down the hallways of the building. Cole was offered words of good bye by his fellows.

"Good luck, Cole!"

"We'll miss you!"

Cole knew some of these sentiments to be less than genuine, although Jenny in accounting had tried to be nice to him at times. Other comments like:

"Fly away BB!"

He took as closer to honesty.

Cole awoke the next day to find Roy in bad shape. He decided a trip to the park might cheer Roy up. Roy loved the park. He gingerly placed his friend in his pocket and headed out of the apartment.

How he and his friend were going to survive without a job, was unclear to Cole. There were all those nasty things like bills, and rent to pay.

Roy didn't respond well to the park, so Cole decided they should maybe head home. He needed to stop by the grocery, though, to pick up some food.

Cole and Roy walked the streets of the city. Cole let Roy ride on his shoulder, a perch Roy used to prefer on similar excursions. He didn't know why, but Cole decided today to take a different route to the grocery, one that led down an unfamiliar street.

They passed a book store that sold antique books. Cole loved books. He would spend most of his free time reading, with Roy nested in one of his sweaters, or maybe a sofa cushion. They peered through the windows of the small shop to behold all of the rare books displayed in the window case.

Over to the side of the window was a sign, 'Help Wanted'. Cole needed a job. He decided to step inside.

Inside the shop, Cole greeted the lady behind the counter and inquired about the Help Wanted sign. The lady bade him sit in one of the reading chairs the store provided for customers and she would be right with him. Cole settled into the soft leather chair and awaited his interview.

"Hi, I'm Ida Allen. I own this store."

"Nice to meet you. I'm Cole Palmer."

"Hi Cole. Tell me why you want to work here."

Cole was not at a loss for words. He loved literature of all kinds. He talked for what seemed like hours but was probably more like minutes about the books he had read. The adventures. The loves lost and gained. The overcoming of good over evil. Tales of the human condition.

Ida Allen was impressed. There was one thing , however, she needed to know.

"Why did you leave your last job?"

Cole had feared this question. He had to tell truth. "They let me go."

"Why?"

"Well it's probably better if I show you rather than try and tell you."

Cole pulled Roy out of his pocket, and cupping the emaciated bird in the palm of his hand, proffered the bird to Ida for inspection. "They never could understand my friend, Roy."

"Oh, I see."

Now what Ida saw in front of her was a young man with a deep abiding love of books, and an impressive imagination. She saw nothing in the palm of Cole's hand, but then again she saw little worrying there either. She had found, in her experience, most sensitive souls had their little 'quirks'.

"When can you start?"

Roy perked up at that question. He gave a small chirp.

"Tomorrow? Really anytime you need."

"Tomorrow it is!"

They talked about compensation and working hours, but Cole and Roy left he shop with not only a new job, but a sea of books from which to draw. Cole was ecstatic. Roy's eyes brightened, he was excited for his friend.

The days that followed found Cole and Roy getting to the shop early, before Ida showed. They couldn't wait to get working. They dusted the inventory, took care of customers and, in their free time, read. They loved their new position.

Roy was even getting better. The color had returned to his feathers, and he had stopped molting. Cole smiled as the little bird flew from shelf to shelf in the shop, singing all the while. His buddy was back, and in full throat.

There was one particular customer, a regular customer, of the shop that held the most interest for Cole. A young lady named, Kaley. Cole and Kaley would spend hours talking about books. Cole looked forward to their discussions. He probably would have worked there for free, if it meant he could talk to her.

One particular morning, Kaley and Cole were embroiled in an animated debate about the meaning behind the doorstop in the short story, 'Artifice and Practice'. The debate was friendly and fun. The pair ended the discussion with laughter and some good-natured name calling.

Roy saw the pair and wanted to make his ideas known. He flew down from the shelves and hopped onto Cole's shoulder. He leapt into a song that would have made Mozart cry.

"What a beautiful song!" Kaley tilted her head back to better hear the avian symphony filling the small shop.

"And what a pretty shade of Yellow! Is he yours?"

Neurotic Robotics

Traffic was fierce outside the apartment building. Pedestrians filled the sidewalks, rushing back and forth in a lockstep dance. A police siren wailed in the air, as autumn's crisp chill made the passersby pull their coats tighter.

A van, labelled on the side with 'AR', pulled to the curb in front of the apartment building. A man stepped outside the van and opening the large door at the rear of the vehicle, pulled a large wooden crate from out of the van. He loaded the crate on a two-wheeler and pulled his burden into the lobby of the building.

Jason Wright had been waiting six months for this delivery. He had taken a vacation day from work just to be there when the package arrived. Looking out of his apartment window, he witnessed the Allied Robotics van's arrival, and he got a glimpse of the wooden crate that was even now making its way to him.

Allied Robotics was the nation's leader in robotics for the home. He had researched his choice extensively. He was laying out a year's wages for this robot, and he wanted to get the perfect one. He was still watching at the window when the knock came to his door.

Jason opened the door and invited the delivery man inside. The driver gingerly lowered his cargo onto the floor. He wanted no damage to this fragile package. His ability to be promoted depended on him keeping his safe delivery streak going.

Jason thanked the driver and, punching a few icons on his wrist device, both acknowledged the delivery and gave the driver a tip. He almost slammed the door on the deliveryman, as he exited the apartment, he was so eager to open his treasure.

The crate was sturdy by design to prevent any kind of damage to its precious insides. Jason pulled the metal crowbar provided on the crate and endeavored to pry the lid open. Fourteen connectors later, he accomplished his goal and the crate gave up its hold on the contents.

Allied Robotics provided a step by step unpackaging and startup tutorial, in video form, that Jason opted to display on his entertainment wall. A rather smarmy young lady in AR uniform materialized on the wall and began her presentation.

"Welcome to the world of home based automation!"

She carried onward and described all of the modules that should be found in the crate, along with a strategy how to organize and assemble the pieces. Jason followed the instruction faithfully. He had spent a fortune on this chunk of metal, plastic and silicon, and he wasn't about to mess up the installation of it in his home.

Hours passed by in what seemed like minutes. Jason clicked leg assembly A into torso slot C. Arm assembly A was slated for torso slot A. He found the battery for the automaton and following the video, plugged it into its charging station while he finished the rest of the assembly.

The sun was falling over the horizon when he finished his project. He retrieved the battery and installed it in the housing supplied. He pushed the blue button at the bottom of the neck of the robot and waited. The robot vibrated and beeped. The external lights flickered. A few minutes later the machine pulled its head up straight and talked.

"Hello."

Success! He fired up the programming module of the starter videos and in no time he had the robot calling him 'Sir' and roaming the apartment to familiarize itself with the contents.

Jason sat back on the sofa and marveled as his mechanized butler/house maid rummaged through all of the drawers and cabinets in the apartment. He had decided to give the robot the name, 'Jeeves', as an homage to his love of early cinema.

"Jeeves, bring me a coffee won't you?"

"Of course, sir!"

Jeeves was off and running. He whisked into the kitchen and in a flurry of motion, configured the coffee maker to brew a cup.

"Excuse me, sir, but how do you take your coffee? Milk? Sugar? Other additives?"

"Just milk, please. Make it look like deep caramel."

"Right away, sir."

Jeeves spent his time waiting for the coffee, cleaning the kitchen. He picked all of the dishes out of the sink and loaded the dishwasher. He not only dried the sink but polished it and the faucet to a glistening shine. He was about to tackle rearranging the cabinet contents for higher efficiency when the coffee machine completed the cycle.

"Your coffee, sir." Jeeves handed the cup to Jason. "Oh, and I took the liberty of providing some biscuits as well."

Jeeves must be in British mode, Jason figured.

Jason was delighted with his purchase. A clean kitchen sink, a cup of coffee and cookies! Life was going to be easier for him from now on!

Jeeves interrupted his reverie by sticking his right hand under Jason's chin and actuating his vacuum function. There were cookie crumbs on Jason's shirt, but after a thorough wiping of the area, the crumbs vanished.

"That's OK, Jeeves." Jason didn't necessarily need the crumbs removed in such a hurried fashion. "You can clean it later."

Jeeves frowned. "Never, sir!" He finished his attack on the crumbs and sped back to the kitchen to revisit the cabinet reorg.

Confident that his new friend would clean up his mess, Jason put his empty cup on the coffee table and retired to the bedroom. He had had a full day assembling his Jeeves, and all he wanted now was some rest and maybe some video entertainment.

Before he could turn the bedroom light on, Jeeves was pushing past him into the room.

"Bedtime, sir? Shall I pull out your bed clothes?"

"That's OK Jeeves, I can manage."

"Never, sir!" Jeeves was already rummaging through the drawers he had inventoried, and retrieved a set of pajamas with pink roses on them. They were pajamas Jason's mother had given him years ago. He never wore them, in fact he preferred to sleep in his underwear. Jeeves insisted, so he donned the hideously gaudy bed wear and plopped into bed.

Jason drifted off to sleep to the sounds of his busy bee humming in the kitchen, coupled with the drone of his bedroom's entertainment wall. He was happily in a subconscious land of wonders when he was abruptly shaken awake.

"Sir, I seem to have found a problem."

"What?" Jason was confused. He was still a little in dream state, but the bigger question was why Jeeves was waking him. "What's the problem?"

"It seems you have two different sets of dishes." Jeeves looked genuinely concerned.

"What?" Jason did not look genuinely concerned. "Why did you wake me for that?"

"Well, sir, I didn't know how to resolve the issue."

"Could it have waited for morning?" Jason was losing patience.

"Absolutely, sir. Get some rest." Jeeves smiled a worried smile and left Jason to get himself back to sleep.

It wasn't long afterward that Jason was roused from his slumber again. Jeeves was in his bedroom and vacuuming with the vacuum cleaner while dusting with a feather duster. The energetic robot moved with a purpose.

"Jeeves. I'm trying to sleep here!" Jason was getting perturbed.

"Of course, sir." Jeeves made a last run through the carpeting with the sweeper and left the room, closing the door behind him.

Jason sighed. He lay back down on his pillow and tried again to get some sleep. He wouldn't manage to get completely to sleep, this time, before he was awakened yet again.

He was steamed. Jeeves was about to remark, 'Sir...", when Jason reached around to the back of his neck and pushed his power button. The animated machine immediately slumped into a limp tower of gears, motors and silicon chips. Jason pushed the inanimate automaton to its charging station.

To Jason's great surprise, his much anticipated house butler/maid burst into his bedroom again and again all the night. The power button seemed to act more like a reboot button than a power down button. Jason abandoned all ideas of sleeping.

In the morning, Jeeves assembled all of the necessary accoutrements that Jason needed to get ready for work. The robot wanted to help Jason in the shower, but Jason adamantly refused help, telling the robot to reorganize the silverware instead. Cleaned and shaven, Jason ran from his apartment refuge in this world, and caught a transport pod for work.

At work, Jason filed through his contacts and found the Allied Robotics link. He fired off a chat with their customer service.

AR: Hello. How may I help you?

Jason: I'm having trouble with my DY8600E

AR: I see. I'm sorry you are having trouble with our product. May I ask with whom I'm chatting?

Jason provided the appropriate personal information.

AR: OK, I have your records now. I see you purchased our latest model in our home automation line. What exactly is the problem you are experiencing?

Jason: It won't leave me alone. It's always cleaning something and asking questions.

AR: I see. I'm sorry you're having this problem, sir. You are aware, though, that our DY8600E is designed to clean your personal spaces and provide support help for your daily needs?

Jason: Yes, I know. That's why I bought it, BUT … It's driving me CRAZY!

AR: I see. I'm looking at your configuration settings for the unit and I'm noticing that you have it on 24 hour watch. Did you want it to give service around the clock?

Jason: Aha! I didn't know that was an option. Can you set it to shut off or something around 9 PM?

AR: Of course, sir!

Jason was getting suspicious of exactly with whom he was chatting. The customer rep sounded suspiciously fairly similar to his home based stress inducer, Jeeves.

AR: I've also noticed that you have it set for our super clean mode. This mode requires the unit to not stop the cleaning cycles until all forms of unwanted substances have been removed from the domicile.

Jason was sure now that he was talking to some kind of AI.

Jason: Aha again! Could you please set that a little lower for me please?

AR: Of course, sir!

Jason logged off the chat session confident that his home automation problems were now a thing of the past. He finished his day in peace and left work a little early; he was exhausted from lack of sleep.

Jason arrived home to find his robot laying on the couch watching his entertainment wall.

"S'up dude?" The robot rolled over to get a better glimpse of his master.

"What's going on here!?" Jason was confused. His butler/maid acted more like his college roommate. "And why is this place such a mess!?"

"Oh, sorry dude. Got caught up in Volleyball Diaries." The robot pointed to the wall where a group of bikini clad beauties were sitting in a circle arguing over who had taken whose man, and what b*tch they were going to slap.

"Ugh." Jason wiped his forehead.

This was probably worse than before. The apartment was in shambles. There was clothing everywhere and, he knew not why, but his kitchen pans had been displayed in the middle of the living space tangled in the spokes of his bicycle.

Jason fired up the configuration app for his Jeeves on the wall and scrolled through the options. He found the cleaning specificity submenu and noted it had been set to 'Surfer'. He upgraded that to 'Felix Unger'. He waded through the activity options and noticed he could specify privacy levels. He selected 'Unabomber' for that.

He saved his selections and immediately noticed a change in his mechanical servant. Jeeves jumped from the sofa and started collecting the rather large array of clutter from the floor. He whirred and buzzed around the apartment silently. Not a single question came Jason's way.

Having sorted the clutter, Jeeves next entered the kitchen.

Jason tried to relax on his couch, but the racket from the kitchen was a little distracting.

"Can you keep it down in there?"

There was no response from his robotic companion. The clatter continued until suddenly, Jeeves broke out from the kitchen area purveying a stack of plates and cups. He plopped the dishes on the dining table and returned to the kitchen.

There on the table lay what Jason guessed was his dinner. There was a plate of Brussel sprouts swimming in a sea of grease. A side plate held two anchovies with shavings of sliced lettuce.

Jason called into the kitchen. "What the heck is this!?" He received no response.

Jason had had it. This wasn't going to work either. He sat back down in his living area and started up a chat with AR customer service again.

AR: Hello. How may I help you?

Jason: It's not any better.

The customer rep and Jason proceeded to give their back and forth trying to fix the problem. The rep altered the robot's setting in real time so Jason could see the effect the selections made in the robot's behavior. It took quite a while to get it right, but eventually Jason liked what he saw in his new friend.

Jason spent the night in relative ease. His butler/maid took care of all that needed doing so he could concentrate on relaxation.

Jeeves asked if he wanted anything to drink and Jason replied with, "Wine?" Jeeves ambled to the kitchen and concocted what to

Jason would be probably the best glass of Sangria he had ever tasted. The variety of fruit, along with the deep tones of the wine and brandy that Jeeves used, was delightful. It was pure ambrosia to a man who had been stressed for days without sleep.

And sleep was next. Jason was able to prepare himself for bed without any interference from the butler. He even selected his favorite gym shorts for bedclothes. Teeth brushed, Jason sank deep into the cushion that was his mattress and drifted off to what a he expected to be a night of much needed slumber.

Slumber was not to be. Just minutes into his rest, he was awakened by Jeeves.

"Sir, the refrigerator cooling system needs polishing and we've run out of Quintex-Z!"

Jason rubbed his eyes. He thought they were past this. He pushed past his robot and fired up the configuration app once more. All of the setting he had so laboriously set with the customer rep had defaulted back to the original values. He visited the history section and there it was. There had been a power surge.

"Sir, the Qunitex-Z?"

Jason ignored the robot and made his way to his hall closet. He rummaged around a bit and, finding that which he was looking, he turned to the robot and with a mighty swing brought the baseball bat in his right hand up under the chin of the automaton, severing the head of the unit from the body. Jeeves immediately slumped to stillness.

Jason threw the bat on the floor and headed for the bedroom. He would get some sleep now for sure. He drifted off into the arms of Morpheus, hopefully never to awaken.

Five minutes later, a headless Jeeves entered the bedroom.

"Sir, the Quintex-Z?"

The Werewolf Hunters

One

Jake Barton and his friend Ray sat quietly, where Ray's front porch used to be, sitting in lawn chairs and sipping beer. Ray's front porch was currently on the bottom of the Ohio River but that, as they say, is another story. The boys languished in the fading summer days philosophizing and pontificating on the issues of the day while the cicadas chirped their symphonies and the fireflies lit the night with their incandescence.

"You know Ray Ray, I was thinking." Jake was always scheming something.

"You was thinkin'? I didn't know you could do that!" Ray laughed. Jake scowled.

"Ha Ha. I'm serious now." Jake gave Ray that facial expression that quiets laughter. "I seen somethin' on TV the other night that got me to thinkin'."

"Well you better out with it then I guest." Ray loved his friend like a brother and looked up to him as the smarter of the duo.

"Well it seemed to me that there is one whole heck of a lot of TV shows now that's got themselves rooted in what they's callin' reeee-ality." Jake emphasized the RE in reality. He thought it gave it a more 'classy' intonation. "You know, shows about real folks with real lives and such."

"Um hmm." Ray nodded acknowledgement.

"Well the way I seen it, we could do that too. I bet those folks is making millions off'n the lives of ordinary folks and they aint no two more ordinary folks than you and me I guest!" Ray pondered that last part.

"But what do we know about making a TV show?" Ray stated the obvious.

"That's just it! We make a show about somethin' real. Aint no need to write no script or hire no actors, we cain do it all!"

"Well bein' as how I aint never got no actin' lessens, how in the world am I agonna act right?" Ray was unsure of the feasibility of the plan.

"Well then you aint goin' to do the actin' then is you? I is agonna be the star of this here show!"

Jake took some time to let that sink in with his buddy. Ray got that look on his face that said he was 'afigurin', his forehead all scrunched up, and his lips pursed. Finally after an adequate time of cogitation, Ray said, "How is you agonna film this here show? You ain't got no camera!"

"Well you's got one of them there faincy phones aint you?" Jake laughed that Ray didn't know the obvious.

"You agonna film it with my phone?" Ray didn't get the connection. "I don't think it cain do that."

"Your phone has not only got a camera, it cain take video, you faincee phone buying, dipsy doodlin' dummy!" Ray didn't like it when Jake called him a dummy. He may not be the brightest tool in the shed, but he 'weren't no dummy'.

The boys continued late into the night brainstorming ideas for their reality TV show. They considered filming Jake at his job at the

Walmart but that didn't seem interesting enough. Ray suggested they do some kind of fishing show but Jake didn't like that, they'd have to actually catch fish to make it interesting. They went back and forth trying ideas on each other with no success. Finally Ray brightened, "Hey, did you hear about Mavis Green?"

"The Mavis that lives out on 425N?" Jake looked interested.

"Yes that the one. She had one of her sheep kilt yesterday by what some is sayin' were a werewolf." Ray's eyes grew wide at the thought.

"Werewolf?" Jake snickered. "Aint been no werewolfs here since before the big war." Now the big war to Jake was WWII.

"Now hold on there. I talked to Mavis and it seem they got some brown hairs out'n the sheep's mouth. Long and brown like, you know, a werewolf!" Jake seemed unimpressed.

"Well I gots to see it to belief it." Jake mumbled. "That might just make a good TV show though?" Ray looked excited, he hadn't expected Jake to approve any idea he would have. "Less us go an' see Mavis tomorrow after work then?" They agreed on a time.

Later the next day, Jake pulled up to the QuickyLube and waited in the parking lot for his buddy. It wasn't long when out of the shop came a lanky young man in oil stained overalls. Walking to the passenger door, Ray jumped in the F150 pickup.

"You ready to make us some magic?" Jake smiled at his friend.

"You betcha buddy, less go!"

Jake gunned the engine and soon they were leaving the outskirts of their small town and headed into the countryside. They were looking for Mavis Green's farm, it would only take 5 minutes or so to get there. Asphalt road turned to gravel which turned to dirt and they arrived.

Mavis Green was a middle-aged spinster who worked a small farm by herself. She kept a few sheep and pigs and tried to pretty much grow whatever vegetables she needed. Her annual income was very low as her only source of income was selling her surplus pigs and sheep. Jake was the first out of the pickup and, approaching Mavis, extended his hand.

"Hi there Ms. Green."

"Hello." Mavis shook Jake's hand not entirely sure who he was. "Oh hey, Ray!" She saw Ray get out of the truck and hugged the oil soaked young man. "What brings you all out here?"

Ray was about to speak but Jake interrupted. "We interested in yous werewolf attack, coupla days ago." Seeing that met with no immediate negative response, he furthered. "We'd like to interview you for our TV show."

Mavis was positively agog. She had never been interviewed let alone on TV! She could hardly speak but managed to blurt out, "Oh my! But I look a mess!"

"You aint never looked better!" Ray chimed in. "We's doin' a reee-ality show, so's the more real you look the better."

"Well I guest so." Mavis tried to poof her hair with her hands.

"First off, I'd like to see the place where this here attack occurred." Jake was playing director as well as host. Mavis took them out to the field and showed them a large dark brown spot on the grass.

"This is where he got her." Mavis' voice cracked as she said it; the animals were very important to her.

"You getting this on film?" Jake snapped at Ray. He should have already been filming. Jake walked out in front of Ray to the brown spot and began his narrative. "This, my friends, is where the beast struck. One innocent animal lost its precious life to the demon scourge." Then to Ray, "Did you get that?" Ray leaned over his phone and pressed a couple of buttons.

"I think so, why don't you take a gander." Ray handed the phone to Jake.

"You left handed bird brained horse's hind end! You had it on picture mode. All you got here is a picture of me pointing to the brown spot! Lookie here." Jake then explained to Ray again how to set the phone up to take the video. Mavis seemed perturbed that this relative stranger to her should be talking so harshly to someone she knew to be so kind and friendly, Ray. Jake stepped in front of the camera again and said, "Take two."

After numerous takes, and satisfied with the footage by the crime scene, the boys thought it best to get the interview with Mavis at her kitchen table. It would seem more 'homey' Jake thought. Mavis made them all some tea and then, settling down to the table, the interview commenced.

"Where was you when you saw that there Werewolf?" Jake started with the hard hitting question.

"Well I never done actually seen it." Mavis was nervous in front of the camera.

"Well then, why do you think it was a werewolf then?" Jake was beaming with confidence. This was the job he was born to do.

"Well you see, when I came upon the corpse of Tammy. Tammy was the sheep's name that got kilt." Jake sighed a sigh of exasperation. Mavis continued, "Well when I saw Tammy lying there all white and all like all of the blood had been taken *out* of her."

"Wouldn't that be more like a vampire than a werewolf?" Jake was hell bent on getting the facts right.

"Well werewolfs and vampires, they cain both suck the living blood out of you, you know." Ray gave his assessment off camera.

"Who in the hail asked you?" Jake was livid. Hosting was *his* job. "Let's keep going, we can edit that out."

"So the blood being gone was what started your suspicion?" Jake slowly nodded his head as if he had caught her with her own words.

"Yes, that and the brown hairs I found in her teeth. She must have fought back."

Jake turned to Ray. "Cut." Then to Mavis. "Can we see the hairs?" Mavis disappeared into her back room and returned with hairs in hand. Jake turned to Ray. "Action."

"So these are the hairs you found?" Jake fondled the evidence in his fingers for the camera.

"Yes, they were in her front teeth. Poor little thing."

Jake turned to the camera and composing himself in his most serious and somber demeanor addressed the audience. "Well there you have it folks. 'Ear refute a bull' evidence of a werewolf and the mayhem they's can deliver. <pause> Cut."

Two

Jake and Ray were having lunch at the Burger King on Main Street to discuss the taping at Mavis' farm the previous day. Ray had brought his phone and, huddled together over the french fries, they assessed the results. Jake pointed his finger from time to time to give his director's comments to the camera man, Ray. Ray spent his time trying to explain to Jake the limitations of his small lensed camera. Jake beamed with pride as the footage completed; at what they had already accomplished.

"Well I do think we got us one heck of a TV show there!" Jake scanned his friend's face for a confirmative expression. Not getting the appropriate response he furthered. "I would definitely watch that if it were on TV even if it was on at three in the morning!"

Ray fidgeted on his side of the booth. "I think it lackin' somethin'. It's like it aint got it no grav–eee-tass or nothin'."

Jake bristled. "It aint got it no grav-eee-tass do it? I bet one hunded dollars you don't even know what grav-eee-tass means you Greenwood Middle School dropout dumass!" Jake didn't take criticism well.

"Well I may not know what it mean but I do know you aint got any!" Ray didn't like being called a 'dumass'.

The boys sat in silence mulling over their conflict. Finally Jake spoke. "Sorry Ray. I jus' want so bad for this work. "

Ray understood and soon the friends were back planning their next move. How could they make it even better? They talked and ate french fries until their lunch hour was almost over.

"Got it!" Ray had an idea. "We need some of that there eye candy."

"What you talkin' eye candy?" Jake thought he was eye candy galore.

"Most of them shows they got some real pretty girls on there just for the eye candy. Don't matter if they know what they's doin' or what not." Jake nodded, no disputing that. "Well suppose we get us Martha to come be your side kick?" Martha was Jake's wife.

"There is no way in God's holy hell that I'm adoin' that! Martha'd kill me if she knew we was adoin' this!" Ray had to agree, Martha had enough on her plate taking care of her Dad and working a full time job.

Ray thought awhile. "What about Crissy at the QuickyLube?" Crissy was the cashier/receptionist where Ray worked. She was young and unattached and had those physical qualities boys seemed to favor.

"Side kick you say." Jake was considering it. "We could give it a try but if'n she gets pushy, she's out!" Ray agreed.

Back at work Ray approached Crissy with their idea. At first Crissy wanted nothing to do with it but Ray goaded her into it. She had done some theater in high school and had briefly fancied a career as an actress. The harsh realities of life had stifled her dream before it could blossom. Finally she agreed. As Ray had said, she could quit if she didn't like it. Also Ray's offer of 25% of the profits made financial sense. Ray called Jake and the three agreed to do a night shoot on Friday after work.

Friday arrived and Jake pulled his truck up to Mavis Green's farm to find himself alone. He reached into the bed of the pickup and retrieved a crossbow equipped with five arrows. He worked as the manager of the Sporting Goods department at Walmart and he was borrowing the bow. He felt it was a duty; he needed to use the equipment to better be able to recommend it to customers.

Leaning the bow against the truck, he opened the passenger door to reveal a coat and hat laying on the seat. He donned the fedora and looked into the side view mirror of the door to arrange its angularity on his head. He next threw on the leatherette coat and tried it buttoned and unbuttoned in the same mirror to get a feel for which he liked. He was just getting his costume situated when a robin egg blue Ford Focus pulled into the driveway.

"What the heck have you got goin' on here?" Ray was bent over in laughter at the sight of his buddy. "Indiana Jones of Walmart!" His laughter was infectious and soon Crissy was giggling.

"We need us some grav-ee-tass, remember?" This was Jake's attempt at misusing the word.

The trio huddled up with Jake giving the directions to the 'crew'. Crissy didn't seem to like his bossy tone but decided to let it go for now. The plan was they would scour the farm for just the right vantage point and stake out the night looking for the werewolf.

"Over here!" Jake had found something. Crissy and Ray ran to see what it was. "There they are!" Jake standing beside a tool shed pointed to the door.

Ray scratched his head and went in close to get a better look. He tilted his head from side to side observing the area from different angles. Finally he gave up. "I don't see it."

It was Crissy's turn to observe the phenomenon. She had little better luck than Ray. "What is it?" She turned to Jake.

"It's right there!" Jake pointed to the door again. Again the other two failed to see the significance. "On the door! The claw marks!"

To save his buddies bacon, Ray let out a feeble "Oh, yeah." Crissy still couldn't see it. Jake unsheathed a hunting knife from his belt and started enlarging the marks so they could see them better.

Ray figured this was a good opportunity to start filming. He got in close to pick up the fine detail of the carving, then pulled back to get an establishing shot of Jake and the shed. He motioned Crissy to enter the frame and start talking. Crissy began, "As you can see here, we have the unmistaken-able claw marks of the werewolf."

Jake was livid. "Why you filming me making the marks, and why in the heck is she talking off script!"

Ray stopped filming and looked helpless. "I was just thinking."

"Yeah, you were thinkin' alright." Jake finished the claw marks and resheathed the knife. "Now take your thumb out of your …" Jake trailed off seeing as there was a lady present.

The crew got their footage of the claw marks finally, and set to find a place to wait for the werewolf. Crissy suggested they sit behind some hay bales stacked up by the fence as the bales would make for comfortable seating. Jake wasn't having it and so chose a muddier, thorn infested place at the far end of the farm. The trio sat in silence.

Ray had had a hard week. He had actually done twenty three oil changes just that day. It was no surprise, then, that as the sun sank lower in the sky, Ray sank lower into his seat in the grass. The lower he sank the heavier his breathing became until for all intents he started snoring. Jake pushed his pal over and stopped the noise.

Crissy was getting perturbed. Not only did she not have any lines in this production so far, she hadn't been advised to dress warmly. The colder it got the less enamored she became of being a part of the 'Werewolf Hunter' TV series.

It was becoming very dark now and the moon was rising over the trees on the horizon. The stillness of the night was broken only by the occasional spoosch from a can; equalizing its pressure with the world outside, and providing access to the foamy amber liquid contained inside. Jake thought he heard a noise in the distance. "You hear that?" The others pricked their ears to try and hear it also.

Ray pointed due west. "There." They focused their attention westward and were rewarded by a rumbling in the bushes at the westernmost fence line of the farm. There at the edge of the woods the unmistakable outline of a canine muzzle presented itself. Jake motioned the others to stay put. He slowly reached behind him and pulled his crossbow to his shoulder.

"Quick, give be a quarter." Jake put his hand out to Ray for the coin. Ray fished in his pocket and pulled out his change: no quarter.

"Aint got one." Ray showed Jake the coins.

"Anything silver then!" Jake actually yelled in a hushed whisper. Ray gave him a dime.

Jake jammed the silver coated coin into the business end of one of the arrows and rammed it home into the housing of the crossbow, ready for firing. Ray was confused. "Why the ..."

Before he could complete his question, Jake blurted out somewhat too loudly, "They can only be kilt with silver, dummy!"

Jake motioned to Ray to stop asking questions and get the phone camera going. Ray shoved the phone right to his face to try and get an idea of what the camera was actually capturing. Crissy saw her moment and face in the camera described the scene.

"We're seeing the snout of a werewolf over there in the bushes." She pointed to the spot with the grace of a Price is Right model. "Jake is going to try and kill the monster with his crossbow."

Jake started crawling down the fence line trying to get a closer shot at the beast. Ray and Crissy watched on with feverish anticipation. Jake neared the bush and as if on cue out of the brush jumped a thirty to forty pound canine. Jake fired off a shot but the dime encrusted arrow flew high past the little guy. The dog creature then turned and ran back into the woods not to be seen again.

"Did you get that?" Jake was atwitter with excitement.

"Got it all!" Ray restarted the video for all of them to watch.

Now the video they watched was very dark and grainy. It was hard at times to see what actually was happening, there being very little light. Jake would gloss over those moments. "We can edit that." Then they came to the appearance of the werewolf.

"There it is!" Jake pushed the others away so he could see better. "It's the werewolf of a midget!"

Crissy gave her assessment. "It looks a whole lot like a coyote to me."

Jake laughed. "You never seen a midget werewolf afore has you?" Crissy had to agree she hadn't.

"I have seen a coyote afore, though, and it looked an awful lot like this one."

Ray was next. "I don't think you can all it a midget. I think they like to be called 'Little People'."

"Well call it what you want but that there was one small little person hound from hell!" Jake was still quivering. "I almost got it too!"

Ray commented that the little person werewolf was so far away you could hardly see it. It looked like a small rock in the middle of a giant field. Jake was convinced they could fix that with editing though.

Crissy was fed up. She'd had enough of these Jokers and their stupid TV show about hunting coyotes. She waved them goodbye and don't bother me again and sped off in her robin egg blue Focus.

Jake gave Ray a ride home and could not contain himself with the progress they were making. "We have got to capture us that there werewolf!"

Three

The next day found Jake and Ray hauling used pallets to the woods just north of Mavis Green's farm. The work was exhausting even with the cool autumn temperatures. The boys labored into the afternoon taking a break when all of the wooden merchandise beds were stacked in the small clearing they had chosen to build their werewolf trap.

Jake put down his beer and got up from the log he had chosen for his stool, and pulled a giant spool of baling wire out of a bag.

"Whatcha gonna do with that?" Ray was unsure of its purpose.

"This here is how we's agonna put our trap together." Jake was proud of his engineering idea.

The would-be TV producers set to making the cage that would eventually house their quarry. They positioned each pallet perpendicular to the one next, and affixed them by wrapping baling wire around and around; tying one board on one pallet to a board on the other. When they had five pallets thus secured they admired their work, a perfect box.

"She's nice and sturdy." Jake gave their construction a test shake.

"Ain't no pygmy werewolf gonna break out of that for sure!" Ray was proud of his friend and his flair for creative artifice and outright chicanery. The werewolf didn't stand a chance.

"How we gonna set the trap door?" Ray couldn't conceive of the mechanism needed.

"Well watch and marvel at the wonder that is Jake Barton." Jake smiled and winked to his old friend.

Jake then proceeded to attach yet one more pallet to the build. He only attached on side so that it could swing like a door. He then flipped the box on its side so that the door faced outward that something might walk into it. He searched the forest floor and having found the right stick he propped the door open with it. He stopped to assess the situation.

"We need a trigger." Jake rubbed his chin.

An idea springing to mind, Jake fashioned a smaller stick to hold the larger stick in place but very precariously. He tested his idea with a third stick, gently moving the small stick. With a mighty whoosh the door slammed shut.

"Got him!" Jake heralded the eventual end of their adventure. The boys did a little dance in celebration of their success. "Now to bait the trap."

"What we gonna use?" Ray didn't know what attracted werewolves.

"Less git to the A&P and see if'n we can find us somethin'." Jake was already hiking back to the car.

"We about out of beer too." Jake and Ray didn't like to run out.

After a stop at the beer aisle of the A&P, the boys searched the store for just the right enticement for a man-beast straight out of the gates of hell. Ray wandered over to a display of Ho Hos.

"Hey! How about these?"

Jake was unimpressed and rolling his eyes exclaimed, "You corn fed excuse for a mule! That ain't no kind of food for a werewolf!"

Ray was a little hurt by the chastisement; he loved Ho Hos and what the werewolf couldn't eat, they could. He snuck a box of the delicious chocolate cakes into their cart. Masking his subterfuge he asked. "Well what then!?"

Jake pushed their basket to the meat counter. There arrayed on little plastic trays wrapped in cellophane were treats no blood thirsty rage crazed demon could resist. He pulled a rump roast out of the refrigerated case and examined it. It was nice and fresh. It would make good bait. He looked at the price, $28.59. He put the roast back. "Let's try the 'Manager's Discount' bin."

The store had a case devoted to meat that didn't sell and was getting close to its expiration date. That is, those cuts that couldn't be ground into hamburger to extend its saleable life. Jackpot! Jake pulled a bucket of bloody looking organs from the bin. "$4.59! That's more like it!"

Ray peered over his buddy's shoulder. The bucket was chicken livers. He was confused why werewolves would desire chicken livers. Every chicken liver he'd ever tasted had been nasty.

"How's chicken livers agonna attract any werewolves?"

Jake turned to his pal and explained. "Well chicken livers is full of blood, right?"

Ray couldn't deny that. "Yep."

"And blood is red, right?"

"Yep."

"And don't red blood show up as black in the moonlight?"

"I don't know, do it?" Ray hadn't ever seen blood in the moonlight. And come to think of it, Ray had never seen blood that wasn't red. He guessed werewolves must like black blood or something. That's the best he could make out. He decided to leave it at that. Come to think of it though, Ho Hos looked black moonlight or sunlight.

Up front they paid for their items, well, Ray paid for the items. They were making their way to Jake's pickup when Jake elbowed Ray in the ribs. "Look!"

Out in the parking lot the guys spotted what looked like a little person loading groceries into the trunk of his Camry. Ray turned to Jake. "Huh?"

Jake motioned Ray to hush and in whispered tones dealt out the logic that could not be refuted. "That werewolf we got on tape, what was it?" Ray didn't quite know how to respond. Jake continued. "It was one of them midget werewolfs!"

Ray corrected him again. "They like to be called Little People."

"Yes, yes. Little person werewolf." Jake sighed. "And what is that over yonder?"

Ray couldn't deny it. "A little person?"

"Correcto Mundo." Jake was in a zone. "And how many little people did we have in town afore we had any werewolfs?"

"Well I ain't rightly never seen one I guest." Ray never had.

"So why is it we suddenly got us a little person right nigh about the time we got us a midget werewolf?"

"Little person werewolf."

"Oh yeah. Seem awful coinkidential don't it?"

Ray couldn't argue with that. Maybe this was the werewolf they sought.

Jake motioned to Ray to beat it for their pickup. The boys threw their bags of A&P's finest into the bed of the truck and sped out of the parking lot just in time to pull up behind The Camry with a latent unturned hound from hell driving in the driver's seat. The boys followed him halfway across town to the quiet neighborhood the werewolf suspect called home.

Jake parked the pickup two houses down from their prey and jumping out of the driver's side reached into the bed of the truck and pulled out a large duffel bag. He unzipped the bag and dumped its contents of tools into the truck's bed. He waved Ray to come follow him and putting his finger to his mouth indicated the silence that would be needed for the operation.

The duo slowly crept to the back of the Camry parked in the werewolf's driveway. The, as yet unrevealed monster, exited the house and was coming back for the last bag of groceries from the car's trunk when the boys pounced. Jake jammed the bag over the little man's head and Ray pulled on the zipper trying to get it closed.

Their captive did not cooperate. Like a cat in a bath tub the man gave it his all, kicking and scratching and yelling at full throat. Not wanting to be discovered in their covert action, Ray eyed a shovel resting at the side of the neighbor's house. He picked up the tool and with a mighty swing silenced the dynamo in the bag.

"Put that away!" Jake was livid. "We need him alive to film him changing into the werewolf!" Jake knew the sacrifices that needed to be made for success and fame, but he also knew they needed a live werewolf not a dead one.

They wrestled the bag and its prisoner back to their truck and sped off.

Four

Being a litttle person, Bob Beliot had had many obstacles in life to overcome. There were the obvious physical barriers that a taller world imposed on him, but what was largely unseen were the many preconceptions tall people had for little people. Bob had spent a lifetime battling those preconceptions to be taken seriously.

Bob entered the civilian service for the military right out of college. He was a bright young mind and quickly climbed the ranks, becoming a leading expert in counter terrorism. He spent eight years as an advisor to the US Army on Iraq and Afghanistan before being recruited by the FBI to travel the country advising local municipalities on their terrorism readiness.

He enjoyed the travel and meeting with the various law enforcement agencies. He had made some good friends along the way. He hoped that his hard won expertise in the field might make a difference in the lives he visited.

He pulled his Camry into the little town Jake and Ray called home. The Police Station was right downtown and Bob had no trouble finding it. He stepped out of the car and grabbing his briefcase, headed for the Sheriff's office.

Sheriff Jason Davis was sitting behind a massive wooden desk, shuffling paper around, when Bob knocked on his office door.

"Sheriff Davis?" Bob poked his head inside the door.

"Ah, you must be Mr. Beliot? From the Governor's office?"

"Actually, I'm a contractor." Bob didn't want to be identified as a government drone.

Bob spent the day in the Sheriff's company being introduced to the staff and getting up to speed on their SOP's. The Sheriff's department had four employees: Sheriff Davis, Officers Clark and Holmes, and their gal Friday who pretty much ran the operation, Sally.

"Nice to meet you all." Bob shook hands all around.

"We'd like to give you a tour of our town. You know, to get you acquainted?" The Sheriff motioned to Clark. "Clark, here will be your guide."

Bob and Clark piled into Clark's cruiser and set out. They did a quick circle of the town square and then headed out of town.

"Who maintains your water supply?" Bob wanted to start with the basics. "Also I'll want to see the electric grid."

Clark drove them to the water treatment facility. They drove up to the front door and entered uninterrupted.

"Where are the workers?" Bob was confused at the apparent lack of human presence.

"Well Billy's Mom ain't feelin' too good so he's over at the nursin' home."

Bob was unimpressed. "So where's the surveillance cameras?"

"Well..." Clark didn't know if he was supposed to be embarrassed or not. "I don't think they got any."

Bob grunted. They took a short walk around the grounds. "I've seen enough."

Clark next drove them to the offices of the electric company. They found no one home here also.

"Does anyone do any work in this town?" Bob was incredulous.

"Not if'n they cain hep it!" Clark tried to lighten the mood with a joke. It wasn't well received.

"OK, let's visit the fire station." Bob climbed into the police car.

"Well…" Clark was having a hard time of it. "We ain't got one."

"No fire station?" Bob bowed his head and chuckled the chuckle of 'I'm getting too old for this crap'. "What do you do if there's a fire?"

"Well we mostly just call Piney Valley to send one of their trucks." Clark rubbed his neck, this out of town expert was going to make life miserable for him, he could tell. "We do have us a cracker jack volunteeeer force, though." Clark emphasized the 'teeeeer'.

Back at the station, Bob spent some time talking to the sheriff. There were all kinds of holes in their readiness plan. There was serious work ahead.

"Well we ain't had no kind of problem with terrorism up 'til now." The sheriff was annoyed that the State would send him this irritation. They had gotten along very well, thank you, without outside help. "We ain't even had a murder in town since 1903!" Sheriff Davis was proud of their record.

"Well I know that may be, sheriff." Bob put on his game face. "But the world is changing in some very serious ways." Bob reflected on the horrors he had personally witnessed. "Now those horrors you see on the news may never have gotten to your town, yet. But I am going to do everything my power to see that your town is prepared if it ever should!" Bob stared the sheriff straight in the eyes.

"Ok, Bob, we'll play it your way." Sheriff Davis had his orders from above. "It jus' seems kinda silly to me."

Five o'clock approached and Bob said his farewells. He'd be back bright and early tomorrow to get started. There was a lot that they needed to do to get this town ready.

"We thought if you wanted, you could use the halfway house in town. You know, to get a feel for our friendly community." Sheriff Davis couldn't contain his pride for his community.

Bob welcomed anything that kept him out of another sterile hotel room. "Well I booked a room at the Holiday Inn but that sounds like it'll do." Sheriff Davis gave him the keys to the house and a map to find his way there.

The evening autumn breezes were starting as Bob stopped at the A&P to pick up the essentials he'd need for his stay. The trunk of his car loaded with food and beverage, Bob headed for his halfway house home for the next week or so, unaware that he was being followed. Bob was soaking in the local color, happy being in such bucolic surroundings. 'It sure beats Tora Bora', Bob thought to himself and suppressed a tear in his eye.

Finding the halfway house and using the key the sheriff had given, Bob brought in his bags of A&P goodness. He was making his second trip to the car when he suddenly became aware of a canvas bag of sorts slipping over his head. His counter terrorism training kicked in, and he began hitting and kicking and screaming with everything he had. He knew the first minute of any abduction was the most important. Resist and make yourself heard were his only weapons, his only tools right now.

He felt a strong force hit his face and light up his vision with searing pain. The light faded and all became black.

Five

Meryl Birmingham had lived in the neighborhood for over 80 years. She lived in the house in which she was born. She hadn't liked it very well when the town bought the house next door and made it a halfway house for all sorts of what she thought were 'undesirables'. It was no wonder she rushed to the window when she heard the sound of Bob Beliot's car pulling into the driveway.

Meryl hoped they hadn't rented the place next door out to those 'undesirables'. She had had enough trouble from the former tenant. Her sight wasn't what it used to be, so to her she could just make out Bob carrying groceries into the house as a blur. She tried wiping the dust off of the inside of the window with her hand to get a better look, when she beheld the kidnapping enfolding on her front lawn.

She followed the criminals with her eyes as they loaded Bob into their pickup and left. Faint with fear, Meryl picked up her phone and dialed the police.

Sally was there to dispatch her call. "911, may I have your name please?"

"Why hi Sally. This here's Meryl. Betty May's friend."

"Oh hi Meryl!" Sally knew her as her Aunt's bridge partner. "What's troubling you today?"

"Why I jus' now seen two boys hit another younger boy in the head with my shovel that I was keepin' beside the house to plant my tulip bulbs."

"You saw them hit the man?"

"Yes'm Sally. The one boy hit the other'n pretty hard."

"Are they still there? Are you in danger?"

"Well they took off like a house afire. I don't s'pect they'll be back."

"Ok Meryl. Stay put, I'll have someone come see you."

Sally got on the radio and called for someone to respond to Meryl's call. Officer Holmes was in her neighborhood and so accepted the task. In minutes he was in Meryl's driveway behind Bob's Camry. He noticed the Camry's trunk was open with groceries strewn all along the yard. An inspection of the front door to the house showed it wide open.

Holmes got on the radio. "Sally, see if Bob Beliot is still with the sheriff. I'm here at Meryl's and it looks like someone's in trouble at the halfway house."

Sally responded, "Beliot left here a half hour ago."

Holmes signed off. "Better get the sheriff over here. We got a sit." They used the abbreviation 'sit' for situation.

Holmes unholstered his revolver and entered the halfway house. He shined a flashlight here and there to expose any hidden shadows looming. Finally through with his sweep of the premises he exited the house to find Sheriff Davis inspecting the car.

"Anything inside?" The sheriff was concerned.

"Nothing. No signs of a struggle either."

"Well there's plenty of sign here." The sheriff picked up a carton of ice cream from the ground. "Ice cream still relatively frozen. They can't be gone long."

The police officers walked over to Meryl's door and found her already at the door watching their every move.

"Hi Meryl." The Sheriff knew her. "May we come in?"

"Why sure Jason. Can I make you boys some tea?"

"No ma'am not today. We got some pressing business it look like."

"Why land yes!" Meryl's eyes widened. "You should have seen the ruckus!"

"Tell us about it won't you?"

"Well there I was mindin' my own business like I always do and I heard that there car drive up next door. " Meryl stopped to see if they heard her.

"Yes ma'am, go on."

"Well, don't you know it weren't but two minutes I figger but that there was a holler and a hoop come out of that little boy they beat up under the bag. "

"He was under a bag?" Didn't quite make sense to the policemen.

"He were halfway inside the bag. It were one of them big timey duffel bags. You know, the kind the navy men would use to store they's things."

"Um hmm."

"Well don't you know that the one boy come over to my house and used my tulip shovel to wallop the little boy next door. He walloped him good too cause that poor little thing never did give another peep."

"He wasn't a little boy. He was a little person, ma'am." Holmes tried to get some accuracy into the narrative.

"Why lord o mighty. Do tell! He sure looked like a small young man to me."

"Go on Meryl. What happened next." The sheriff wanted all of the intel.

"Why they zipped the little guy into the duffel and drug him to their truck. The threw him in the front seat and away they flew. I guest that's about it."

"So they was two boys that abducted the little person?" The sheriff summed up.

"Yes. Those monsters! Who goes to hitting another person in the head like that?"

"One last thing. Has you ever seen either of them two boys before?"

"Well it were the older one had one of them hooded sweatshirts on. But he looked Asian to me."

"Asian? Did he have anything wrapped around his head?"

"Well maybe. It was hard to tell with the hood and all ..."

The Sheriff stared into space, lost in thought. "Ok Meryl, thanks for your help. We'll let you know if we need you for anything else."

The men went outside by their cruisers. Sheriff Davis rubbed his chin. Holmes stood at parade rest looking to his superior for guidance.

"Well I think what we got here ..." The sheriff trailed off for a second. "Is that, that so called terrorism expert has done brought terrorism with him to our town. He was s'posed to protect us from it but now he done exposed us to it!"

Holmes nodded agreement. "Those big city types is always tryin' to tell us how to do our job!" Holmes spat on the ground in disgust.

"What's the name of that guy who started working for the Lock and Key factory on 7th street?" Sheriff Davis had an idea.

Holmes looked into the trees until finally the name came to him. "Wasn't it ISIS or Al Qaeda or something like that?

"Get the boys at the VFW and the Kiwanis to meet us at the courthouse. Thirty minutes." The sheriff shook his head. "We got us a terrorist to catch."

Six

Alagarasan Patel had grown up in the slums of Calcutta with his mother and brother. Through the sheer force of his will he had educated himself sufficiently to make it to the USA on a work visa and had landed a job at the Lock Company in town. He was a skilled craftsman and a valued employee who was universally beloved by his coworkers.

Most of his coworkers, however, had trouble with his first name, so they gave him the moniker 'Al'. Some of the more mischievous of his fellows had expanded that to Al Qaeda to tease the gentle Sikh man, much to Alagarasan's chagrin.

Having spent most of his life in one of the densest population center in the world, Alagarasan opted to rent a small house on the outskirts of town deep in the wooded area to spread out and commune with nature. He often meditated in the quiet of his garden, drinking in the spiritual peace he found there.

Unknown to Alagarasan, an entire cadre of police officers and their sworn band of men (with nothing else to do that night) had descended on his little slice of paradise in the woods. Afternoon had given way to evening and the setting sun cast dark shadows everywhere. The men parked their trucks in a semi-circle in front of Alagarasan's house and turning off their engines left the headlamps illuminated to bathe their quarry's hideout in light. The sheriff ordered the house be surrounded to prevent any terrorist escaping. Next, he stormed the front of the house with his deputies.

Alagarasan was busy preparing his dinner when he heard the sounds of cars driving up his driveway. He shut off the stove and was about to open his front door to see who could be visiting him when the front door opened itself revealing Sheriff Davis and his deputies. The men had their weapons drawn and pointed at the fragile man from India.

"On the ground! Hands behind your head!" The sheriff wasn't taking any chances.

While Holmes and Clark subdued and handcuffed the cooperating lock maker, the sheriff started his interrogation.

"Where have you got him?"

Alagarasan was overwhelmed by the turn of events. He raised himself to his knees and pleaded with them. "I am sorry , sir, but I do not know of which you are talking."

The sheriff was growing impatient. "Where is Bob Beliot? We know you and your accomplice took him from his home earlier today."

"I am sure, sir, that I do not know this Bob you are talking about." Alagarasan was adamant. "Please, sir, allow me to explain." This was not the first questioning by the law that Alagarasan had experienced. It was a common event in his years in Calcutta.

"Oh you'll have plenty of time for that where you're going!" The sheriff made a not so veiled threat. "What's that smell?"

Alagarasan looked into the kitchen. "Oh, it's my aubergines." Then to his guests, "Would you like some?" The quiet Indian man would have gladly gone without to provide enough food for his guests.

"Ober jeans? What the heck is that?" The sheriff picked up the pan in which the aubergines were cooking. It looked like a pan of mush to him.

"I am sorry, sir, you might call them the egg plant."

"Who in the world ever heard of sech a thing. A plant that produces eggs? You think I'm stupid!?" The sheriff took it as a personal assault.

"No sir! Definitely not sir!"

"Well egg plant or ober jeans, it look like a mess to me!" The deputies chuckled in solidarity with their chief. "Search the house and the premises." The deputies had their orders.

The deputies and the posse waiting outside the house searched every conceivable hiding place with no results. Some of the party were relegated to interview the neighbors. Some ran their hunting dogs into the woods to see if they could catch a scent trail. Despite the extensive explorations, their efforts left them no closer to rescuing Bob than when they arrived.

Sheriff Davis gathered the men. "Boys, what we got here is a search and rescue mission. There ain't no tellin' where this here terrorist has hid old Bob." The sheriff indicated Alagarasan: Alagarasan winced.

The sheriff then proceeded to pull a ball capout of his back pocket. "Marvin, bring your hunting dogs here." The sheriff gave the blood hounds a sniff of the cap he had retrieved from Bob Beliot's trunk. "Less git to huntin'!"

The crowd roared their approval. They were not going to let the terrorists win; not in their town! Deputy Clark was given the unglamorous task of escorting their prisoner along with them, in case they might need to question him further. Alagarasan plodded along dutifully, ruing the day he decided to come live in this small town.

Deep into the woods the hounds led their mob. The men spread out in a fanning maneuver to cover more ground. The dogs howled and moaned as they followed this trail then that. Finally as if shot from a gun the blood hounds raced into the thickets. They were on the scent for sure now, the boys tried their best to follow.

Over a ridge the troop sped, endeavoring to keep the hounds in sight. At the other side of the hill they stopped. The hounds bayed and snapped at the base of a large maple tree. They were intent on something in the canopy above.

"Aha! We've got your hiding place now Al Qaeda!" The sheriff bristled with confidence as he neared the tree. He had just demonstrated a coup of professional police work. Not hours from the kidnapping had he managed to not only apprehend the culprit who engineered the crime, but he had found the victim.

"Help him get down." The Sheriff motioned to the men to get Bob Beliot out of the tree.

The posse stood around, sheepishly unmoving. A few of the men pointed into the canopy. The Sheriff approached and looked skyward. There in the tree sat a wide eyed raccoon, nervously twitching its tail.

Seven

It was already dark when Jake and Ray returned to their wooden werewolf trap/cage in the forest. They removed the now semi-conscious Bob Beliot from his duffel bag prison and placing him in the cage proceeded to wire it shut with more bailing wire. Their prize now secured the boys admired their handiwork and noticed a flaw.

"How the heck we gonna get any video of him changing' into the werewolf with all of these here slats of wood in the way?" Ray had spotted the error: the pallets they used to make the cage didn't allow much light to penetrate.

"Well, git to pryin' some of them off then!" Jake had better things on his mind. Jake walked into the woods to do some thinking.

Ray spent the better part of a half hour prying boards from their werewolf display case. The sun had gone down and the cool of the night was falling so he decided to convert the unwanted planks of wood into a small fire to keep warm. He was just warming his hands and pulling open a Ho-Ho when a foggy headed Bob Beliot sat up in his cage.

"Where the heck are me?" Bob was disoriented.

"We in the woods north of town, werewolf!" Ray knew how crafty werewolves could be so he wanted to show the beast who was boss.

"Huh?" Bob didn't think he heard that correctly. Bob lay back down and touching his nose found it very tender. "I think you broke my nose!"

Ray inspected the captive. "Yep. You got a lot of blood too." The front of Bob's face was coated in his own blood. Ray pulled an oily rag out of his back pocket. "Here. Clean yoursef up."

Bob reluctantly accepted the rag and, using the cleanest parts of it, wiped his face gingerly being careful to avoid the nasal region. His head was clearing. He had been kidnapped, but why he had been kidnapped remained a mystery.

"What are you guys aiming to do?" Bob looked Ray straight in the face.

"We aiming to show the world that we ain't never agonna stand for no werewolf in our town!"

Bob was caught off guard. He had heard him correctly the first time. "Werewolf?"

"That right. And don't think 'cause you a little person we ain't seen you comin'!" Ray gloated a little over their werewolf hunting skills.

"I got news for you buddy. I'm not a werewolf. There aren't any werewolves, it's a myth."

"Spoken like a true werewolf!" Ray wasn't falling for it. "Tryin' to put us off'n the scent huh!?"

Bob realized he wouldn't get anywhere with this guy. He decided to try some of his anti-terrorism techniques. "Who's the boss here anyway? It's the other guy, right?" He was trying to get the two of them to distrust each other.

"Well I'm the boss of me. Jake's the boss of hisself." Ray leaned back to enjoy his Ho-Ho.

"Those look good, what are they?" Bob pointed to the pastry.

"Them's Ho-Hos."

"Can I try one? I'm kind of hungry." Bob knew folks who ate together formed a bond of sorts.

"Sure." Ray threw him a cellophane wrapped treat. "You want a beer to wash it down?"

"You bet!" Bob had a drinking buddy now.

Jake returned from his reveries in the trees, scripting the next scene of their epic. "Well lookey here, it's the midget and the idgit!" Jake gave a little belly laugh.

"It's little person, you idgit!" Ray was getting tired of correcting his friend.

"OK then. It's the little person, and the idgit for certain!" Jake laughed even harder at his own impromptu witticism. "He h'aint turned yet, has he?"

"Nope."

Jake scanned the bushes and found what he was looking for. He pulled a long dead tree limb from the ground and began poking Bob through the spaces between the slats of the makeshift cage.

"Hey!" Bob squirmed to avoid the punishment. "Stop it you moron!" Bob was getting perturbed.

"What you doin'?" Ray didn't see the point to it all.

"Them werewolfs turn when they gets angry." Jake gave Bob another jab.

The offensive to get Bob agitated had succeeded but had not produced a single werewolf. Jake thought for a minute. "Well less try this."

Jake rummaged through their grocery sacks and found the jar of chicken livers. Having popped the lid, Jake then proceeded to douse their captive with the contents of the jar.

"What the eff did you do that for!?" Bob was getting redder and redder in the face. Red from the chicken liver goo and the blood oozing from his nose, no doubt, but also red from the rage building within him. "Stop that!"

Jake chuckled as he finished pouring the livers. Ray looked at him curiously. "Them livers gonna make him change too?"

"That right. They can't resist the smell of blood."

The boys sat back and waited. It wouldn't be long until their captive made the transition for sure. Jake made Ray keep his camera phone focused on the cage to catch any of the phenomenon he could.

Ray was the first to hear it. It sounded a long way off, but he thought he heard the sound of dogs baying. "You hear that?"

Jake cocked his head to one side and listened. "Yeah buddy." And then. "Thems the gang of hell hounds this little guy been waitin' for. He think they agonna spring him from this here trap."

The sounds got louder and louder until Ray and Jake, fearing for their very lives, raced off into the bushes. They stopped just far enough to miss the deluge of hound flesh about to descend on the camp site, but close enough to be able to document the event with their camera.

They didn't have long to wait. Marvin's dogs had gotten the scent of the chicken livers from across the woods and were flying in formation to catch their quarry. Now, the cage that Ray and Jake had put together had been rickety enough with just bailing wire to hold it together, but when Ray removed the slats for better viewing, he inadvertently weakened the structure even further. The result was that when you mix a pack of hungry hunting dogs with the scent of fresh livers, you don't get much polite etiquette between the dogs and what they are searching.

The dogs piled onto Bob's fragile place of confinement and in so doing, tore it to pieces. Scraps of woods flew in the air as the dogs searched the prison for delicious livers. Bob, having a lot of the chicken goo spread all over his body, got a lot of dog slobber added thereto as the dogs tried to lap as much nutrition as they could.

The sheriff and his posse arrived just in time to pull the dogs off of poor Bob before the dogs could decide to make Bob part of the meal. One of the boys in the posse noticed something shiny in the bushes. It was Ray's camera phone. "Over there! Terrorists!" The entire posse starting firing their guns randomly into the woods.

The sheriff turned and spotted the same glint of plastic and glass. "Cease firing! We want to take them alive boys! We need them for questioning!"

Jake wasn't much of a fighter. He would rather negotiate, but it didn't look like these guys were in the negotiating mood. He tore off running through the dense underbrush, cutting his arms and face as he went.

Ray was a fighter. He lay into the mass of temporary deputies with both fists flailing. He gave as good as he got, and then some. Two of the deputies fell to the ground and started nursing their wounds. The others raced back to get their weapons. 'Take him alive' be dammed! They were going to do it the easy way.

Ray took their retreat as a good opportunity to get out of there. He piled into the brush, trying to find his friend.

↔

Bob Beliot, having regained a semblance of composure, gathered his men around him in the fading campfire light. His first instinct was to strategize a dragnet to capture his nitwit captors and bring them to justice. To do that, however, he would have to admit publicly that he, considered by many to be an expert in anti-terrorism methods, had allowed those mental deficient to kidnap him. He decided on plan B.

"OK sheriff, what time do you have on your watch?"

The sheriff pulled up the sleeve of his shirt and read the time. "One fifteen".

"So if I was captured at approximately four in the afternoon, how long do you think it took you to find me, not farther than a few miles from your office door!?" Bob said the last part loudly for emphasis.

"Less see." The sheriff mumbled some words to himself and finally answered. "Eight hours and fifteen minutes!" The sheriff looked confident.

Bob bowed his head to grieve the life that could have been for him. "You wanna try nine hours?"

The sheriff looked sheepish. "Oh, yeah."

"What the heck have you been doing for over nine hours!? Did you stop for dinner on the way? Did you have to take a nap?

Tell me, sheriff, what in the world would take you so long to find one of your missing officers, just a few miles away!? And to top that off, I wasn't even kidnapped! This was a simulation!"

One of the posse spoke. "A simulation?" Bob gave him a stare that sent the man to looking on the ground for something.

The sheriff was smart enough not to reply. Bob went on for ten minutes, dressing down the entire squad. There was going to be hell to pay for this he promised. Finally having blown off most of the frustration of the night, he turned to the gentle man from India.

"Who is this?"

The sheriff didn't know how to respond. "We thought he might have been the terrorist who grabbed you?"

Bob let out a disgusted grunt. "You did, did you? This man is obviously a Sikh. He's about as radical as your mother's chicken and dumplings." Bob tried to control his anger. "He's as much a terrorist as you are good cops!" Bob pulled one of the deputies from the group. "I want you to take this man home and make sure he gets there safely. Do you understand?" The deputy nodded agreement.

Bob turned to the group. "Let's pack it all up and get back to town. I want everyone at the office by zero seven hundred in the morning. We have a LOT of work ahead of us."

↔

It didn't take long for Ray to catch Jake. Jake hadn't had any exercise in … well let's just say that Jake didn't get much exercise except at the buffet line. The boys were out of breath and looking behind to see if they were followed, decided to take a little break.

"Did you get that on camera?" Jake was agog at the possibilities. The melee had been quite frenetic and he was sure the werewolves had induced the appropriate transformation of their captive.

"Yes I did, but…" Ray looked sheepishly at his buddy. "The phone broke during the fight."

"You unparalleled nincompoop! Your momma musta been a baboon 'cause you ain't got the sense you was borned with!" Jake was mad. "We've lost everything!"

Ray hung his head. Jake hung his too. The boys sat in quiet despair.

Ray was always one to look on the bright side. "Well my cousin Jesse's kid always says …"

Jake snapped at that. "He always says, huh!? I didn't know baboons could talk!"

"Well I think they cain do sign language?" That got a 'hmmph' from Jake. Ray furthered, "Anyway, he says that when your phone gets broken, all your music and pictures go up to the clouds. You know, like to be with the angels … and Jesus."

Jake thought about that. He scratched his chin and looking to the sky allowed a tiny smile to cross his lips. "Your cousin's boy sure said something, all right." Jake's smile broadened. "I bet he may be onto somethin'." Jakes eyes brightened. "I bet folks in heaven is already looking at our video. Theys seein' how we's done our part to rid this here world of all kinds of werewolf evil."

Ray nodded his head. "I bet you right!"

The boys started walking home, this time walking about two feet higher off the ground than before. They rounded Hanson's ridge and stepped onto the highway.

"You know Ray Ray? I'd like to see Reverend Haywood top that one!" Jake was pleased. They laughed. The pair strolled as two fully actualized men: men of substance and purpose: men who had had just pulled off a great success.

Eight

The forest lay quiet as the events of the night ended. A small canine, looking much like a coyote, crept out from its hiding place in the brush. It sniffed around the crumpled pile of pallets and bailing wire, finding a liver here and there to eat. He lay down for rest as the first rays of sunlight kissed the top of the forest trees.

A fog fell over the beast and slowly but surely the animal began to twist and contort itself. The brown fur that had covered the hound before fell to the ground as paws were replaced with hands and muzzle and maw turned to jaw and face.

When the transformation was over, a small child lay on the dewy ground. The lad righted himself on two legs and began his walk home.

43270299R00097

Made in the USA
Middletown, DE
23 April 2019